Patricia Beatty

BILLY BEDAMNED, LONG GONE BY

The American tall-tale tradition provides the inspiration for this rumbustious story about the many exploits of an old Texas cowboy in the person of one Rudd Quiney. As Merle and Graham Tucker listen to their Great-uncle Rudd's wildly embroidered yarns they find themselves both exasperated and impressed.

Everything about Rudd was a surprise, including his existence, for Grandmother had quarrelled with him forty years before and never spoken to him since. She wouldn't say why, but the children quickly discovered that Rudd was a terrible liar. And his biggest whoppers were about how he'd lost his ear. Some were funny, like the one about the hostile pig and the helpful cyclone; some seemed almost believable, like the story of his Civil War campaign; or scary, as when he was captured by Comanches; all had undeniable flair. Yet the true explanation, when it came clear, proved as outlandish as all the others.

With strong, lively characterizations and pithy, colorful language, Patricia Beatty serves up a hearty helping of Americana that is deliciously, rib-ticklingly entertaining.

LY
NED,
NG
BY

BY JOHN AND PATRICIA BEATTY

Holdfast
King's Knight's Pawn
Master Rosalind
The Royal Dirk
Who Comes to King's Mountain?
Witch Dog
published by William Morrow and Company

At the Seven Stars
Campion Towers
A Donkey for the King
Pirate Royal
The Queen's Wizard
published by The Macmillan Company

BY PATRICIA BEATTY

The Bad Bell of San Salvador
Blue Stars Watching
Bonanza Girl
By Crumbs, It's Mine!
Hail Columbia
How Many Miles to Sundown
A Long Way to Whiskey Creek
Me, California Perkins
The Nickel-Plated Beauty
O the Red Rose Tree
The Queen's Own Grove
Red Rock over the River
Rufus, Red Rufus
The Sea Pair
Something to Shout About
Squaw Dog
published by William Morrow and Company

Indian Canoe-maker
published by The Caxton Printers, Ltd.

The Lady from Black Hawk
published by McGraw-Hill Company

J
(10-14)

BILLY BEDAMNED, LONG GONE BY

Patricia Beatty

DIXON PUBLIC LIBRARY
DIXON, ILLINOIS

PBC 5-77 5.86

William Morrow and Company / New York / 1977

120746

Copyright © 1977 by Patricia Beatty
All rights reserved. No part of this book may be reproduced or utilized in any form or by any means, electronic or mechanical, including photocopying, recording or by any information storage and retrieval system, without permission in writing from the Publisher. Inquiries should be addressed to William Morrow and Company, Inc., 105 Madison Ave., New York, N. Y. 10016.
Printed in the United States of America.
Design by Victoria Gomez.

1 2 3 4 5 6 7 8 9 10

Library of Congress Cataloging in Publication Data

Beatty, Patricia.

Billy bedamned, long gone by.

SUMMARY: Two youngsters meet their Uncle Rudd who tells them tall tales about his life with the cowboys, Indians, and Confederates.

[1. Texas—Fiction. 2. Western stories] I. Title.
PZ7.B380544Bi [Fic] 76-55386
ISBN 0-688-22101-7
ISBN 0-668-32101-1 lib. bdg.

Contents

For
Mrs. Carl H. Schultz
and
the "real" Brownie

1

Ready, Set, Go!

"Redheads we were, every blessed one of us Santa Rosa County Quineys! The whole brood of us Texas Quineys ranged from dark auburn through copper to pure carrot red. Not all of us were freckled and speckled as frogs, though some were, but there wasn't a one of us who wasn't redheaded when he was your age, children."

Once a month or so, Grandmother Susannah said those same words to Graham, my brother, and me. She would sit under our green-beaded, front-room lamp embroidering, sigh, and look over her spectacles at the two of us. That look made us feel that we should have had red hair too, instead of brown. Something had gone wrong with us Tuckers. After all, our mother Floy had red hair, and she had been only half a Quiney, Grandmother Susannah's only child. We felt that Grandmother thought that being half Quiney was much better than being only a quarter Quiney like Graham and me. Sometimes we got the idea that she didn't think too much of the pair of us. She liked her little half-Chihuahua dog, Brownie, better.

It wasn't fair of her. We didn't make much noise around the house, and we both got good grades in the Pasadena schools. I was thirteen and a half and in the eighth grade where I got A's, even in arithmetic, though I was a girl. Graham, who was going on eleven, was in the sixth grade and a crackerjack reader and speller, things boys weren't supposed to do as well in as girls. But we couldn't honestly say that we delighted Mom's mother, and the old lady didn't often delight us either.

Graham and I were looking forward eagerly to the summer so we could escape her and go up to Bishop again to stay for a month with our dad's sister and her husband on their ranch near the Sierra Mountains. We'd spent the last three summers with them, and we had had a fine time. They had dogs galore and horses too.

But, darn it, this summer of 1929 promised to be different!

That was because of Mom's car. She'd bought one with her own money and because of that she claimed it wasn't anybody's business but her own. Dad had a 1928 Essex coupe, a dandy little car, but she didn't drive that. She wanted her own car, which had turned out to be a 1923 Studebaker sedan.

Mom didn't give a rap that she couldn't drive. A book of instructions came with the Studebaker, a big black car that had belonged to one of her friends who sold it because she wanted a new Packard.

No one in our family would ever forget the first time Mom took the wheel of the Studebaker. She'd read the instruction book for three days before she slid under the wheel into the front seat, with Graham, me, Grandmother, and Brownie looking on. It was Saturday, and Dad had gone down to his office to get some papers to look at over the weekend. He'd taken the Essex, so the coast was clear for Mom to try to drive the Studebaker, which Mom's friend had driven into our garage for her. Dad hadn't been pleased, because now the Essex had to stay overnight down at the curb. He thought the Studebaker ought to be out there on the street, not his car.

Sitting in the front seat, Mom started to give all sorts of orders to us. She posted me on one side of the driveway and Graham on the other. Grandmother stood on the back porch with Brownie in her arms, so the dog wouldn't rush out and get under the car wheels when Mom backed the Studebaker out of the garage.

"You be careful of that car, Floy," I heard Grandmother calling out to her. She had an arm around the dog and a hand tight around the back-porch railing. She was nervous. All of us were because we'd heard last night's row.

Dad had yelled at Mom about her refusing to learn to drive with someone "qualified" to teach. And she had yelled back that there was no reason to spend the money for driving lessons—not when she had the instruction book. She said it would surely tell her all she needed to know to be a lady motorist, and once she got the hang of driving, there wouldn't be a bit of trouble. Dad had gone off to bed muttering to himself.

Now Mom called from the car, "Stay on the porch, Mother, and don't worry. Merle, you get close to the house and you too, Graham. I'll be coming out any minute."

She came out. She didn't crank the car the way our

neighbors had to crank theirs. Her Studebaker was new enough not to need cranking, except maybe for trouble on the road. Mom's car started up with a roar, not a splutter like Dad's Essex. And then all at once the Studebaker moved, because Mom had put her foot on the gas pedal and had released the brake.

Crash, bang—the Studebaker went out through the front of the garage with boards splintering and breaking over the top of the hood.

"No, Floy, make it go backwards," Grandmother shouted over Brownie's barking.

"Mom, you went the wrong way!" yelled Graham, running forward alongside the garage as the car plowed through it into our backyard.

I waited until I heard the motor stop, then I came up carefully. Grandmother followed behind me, shaking her head. Brownie was at her heels, yapping in excitement.

"Mom didn't do it right," I said to Grandmother.

"No, she didn't. I suspect Floy got a little mixed up in that book. It did seem terribly complicated."

Mom was sitting in the car looking pale. She said, "I think I got mixed up a lot, Mother." I hadn't expected her to admit it, but she did. There were grapevines sprawled out all over the car top, and our wooden latticed arbor was lying smashed over the radiator ornament. She'd hit our cement birdbath head on and knocked it over onto the grass, but it hadn't broken.

As Graham got up on one running board to look in and I got up onto the other one, Mom spoke again to

Grandmother, who was pulling off some grapevines. "I suppose, Mother, that I better do what John says and take a lesson or two on how to drive before we head out for Louisiana in June."

Louisiana? This was the first time I'd heard about going there. "Louisiana, Mom?" I yelped.

She was studying the instruction book again. "Yes, Merle, we've been invited to visit one of your grandfather's cousins in New Orleans."

"The New Orleans Fawcetts," Grandmother said, as if I knew those relations of her husband's.

"But we don't know them," my brother said.

"Then it's time you met them," said Mom. "They are very nice people. Your father says he's going to be far too busy this summer to go anywhere at all, so the four of us are going motoring in my car." She turned to Grandmother. "Please go inside and put the teakettle on. By the time I've mastered this machine enough to back into the garage from here, I'll be needing a cup of tea." Then she spoke to Graham and me. "You two get off the running boards immediately and go to safe places. Take Brownie away with you, Merle. I'm about to reverse as soon as your grandmother is out of the way."

Reverse was what Mom did after I'd grabbed Brownie and run for the side of the house with the dog struggling under my arm. Mom reversed quite quickly. The Studebaker plunged backwards out from under the arbor, and in two jolts, and a scratched fender, Mom was back inside the garage in a sort of crooked position.

"There now," she cried to us, as she switched off the engine, "I did it! I have driven!"

"Yes, sir, Floy, you drove all right." Grandmother was on the back porch now, shaking her head as she watched.

I followed her into the kitchen, where I put her dog down on the linoleum. "Is that how redheads in your family do things back in Texas?" I asked.

Grandmother paused, looking far away into the distance, and said, "Some of us have been known to. You know, sometimes I even think that something of Rudd is to be found in your mother."

"Rudd? Who's that?" The name was new to me.

"Nobody you know, Merle. You can take comfort from that."

I kept on. "Is Rudd a he or a she?"

"Oh, he's a he all right."

"Has he got red hair?" If he was related to Mom, I imagined he had to be a Quiney. I knew all of Dad's people, the Tuckers, because they lived in southern California too. There weren't many of Grandfather's people, the Fawcetts, at all, and I knew them all by name, if not by face. There wasn't any Rudd Fawcett.

Grandmother answered me, saying, "I have no idea what color his hair is or if he even has any, Merle. Now don't you pester me anymore. I want to make the tea and start lunch. Better yet, you get last night's hash out of the icebox and let me warm it up on the stove for Brownie's bowl."

There! She was trying to stop questions by putting me to work, but I kept on, "Will we really be going to New Orleans, or is Mom just saying that?"

"No, it seems that we are really going. Your mother has written your grandfather's relatives accepting their invitation."

"But why won't Dad be coming too?" I knew that he could take some time out during the summer if he wanted to.

"Because he doesn't like the Fawcetts. He says that they are 'yaps.' They talk too much."

"And you don't like Rudd whatever-his-name-is any better, do you? Is he a yap?"

She went over to the sink to fill the kettle. "Merle, you have a way of coming back and back to something, don't you?"

"Is coming back and back like a Quiney?" I supposed there had to be something cropping out in me somewhere that was like her family.

She studied me hard out of sharpened brown eyes. "Yes, it's a trait some of them suffer from. Not all of them, though."

Before I could ask more about who this mysterious Rudd was, the telephone rang out in the hallway. I went to answer it. As I'd guessed, it was our next-door neighbor inquiring about the grape arbor, which had been on her property too. After she'd asked whether we planned to put it up again, and I'd said that I was sure Dad would fix it when he got home, I let her know that she needn't worry about Mom's driving much longer because we were going to Louisiana. Mom was going to drive us there.

"God forbid," said our neighbor. Then she said, "I'll talk to your grandmother over the fence later."

"Sure," I answered, and I hung up. For a time I stood in the hall watching Grandmother as she went to the icebox to get out the hash with Brownie trotting behind her. She was going to feed the dog herself, which was what I'd expected of her. When Grandmother wanted a thing done, she wanted it done right now, not tomorrow, not next year.

I didn't want to go to Louisiana. I didn't want to go anywhere with Grandmother, to tell the truth. She made Graham and me mind her. Mom was more easygoing with the two of us.

I wondered what Dad would say when he came home and saw what had happened to the garage. I dreaded it.

But nothing much really happened. There was some yelling, and I heard him say very loudly and clearly, "the yaps," which had to mean the Fawcetts in New Orleans. After that Mom came running out of their bedroom, shutting the door behind her. She had her purse with her. She opened it, took out her coin purse, opened that, and fished out some change—two dimes and a nickel. She told me, "Merle, go round up your brother, so you and he can have supper in the kitchen with Grandmother. Afterward you kids can go to the picture show by yourselves. Your father and I have some things to settle here, so we won't be going, and your grandmother's playing pinochle across the street. Your father will come after you and drive you home the way he always does."

Alone! To the picture show! Graham would like that as much as I would. And the extra money, that nickel, would buy five licorice whips to suck on! Laurel and Hardy were playing that night, along with a serial about a boy raised in the jungle by a kindly tigress who had lost her own cub. Last week the boy had fallen into a pit of crocodiles, and one was coming toward him with its mouth wide open, showing its teeth. And then, of course, the screen had gone black. Grandmother had been with us then. She said the crocodile was rubber and the serial only a "story," but what she'd said hadn't stopped our pleasure. It was good that Graham and I could be going alone tonight, because last week we'd seen the previews of another serial, one that Grandmother had vowed wild horses couldn't drag her to. It was about a fair-haired princess who'd been kidnapped to another planet and was the prisoner of a cruel king with a man's body but a dragon's head. All of the planet's people had dragon's heads except the palace servants, who had frog's heads. The serial was called *Dolores, Daughter of Doom, Prisoner of the Planet Persephone.* It had sounded good.

I ran out of the house to find Graham. He was still where I'd last seen him, sitting in the front seat of Mom's car, looking at the book of instructions. I got into the back seat, showed him the money, and said, "Mom's sending us to the picture show so we won't hear her and Dad arguing about her accident and our going to Louisiana to visit the Fawcett yaps."

"That's good." He held the book up, showing me a page. "This is all about the clutch and when to use the crank. There's quite a bit to driving a car, I guess."

"I suppose so." Cars did seem to be pretty complicated things. I'd looked under the hood of the Essex and the Studebaker and seen that they were full of machinery. The Studebaker was bigger than the Essex coupe all over. The Essex had a rumble seat, which wasn't at all comfortable for trips to the beach after the first exciting five minutes of riding in the wind. The Studebaker had a big back seat, with silver and glass vases on each side to put flowers in so passengers could smell them while they rode in comfort.

"Do you think we'll really go to Louisiana? Will Dad let us go without him?" Graham looked hopeful that Dad wouldn't agree.

I said, "You'd better give up on going to Bishop. Mom bought this car, though he didn't want her to. She's gone that far. I know she means to go all the way to New Orleans. Maybe it's that Quiney blood in her. And Grandmother, who's all Quiney, has made up her mind to go too. That's two of 'em against us."

"Yes, it looks that way." He was quiet for a minute, studying the how-to-drive booklet. Then he asked, "How long do you think we'll be away?"

"All summer long, I think. Grandmother says we'll leave right after school lets out, and I'll bet we're back in time for the first day of school in the fall. You know how Grandmother is about our missing a single day of school."

"I know. That's what I was afraid of—that we'd be back in time for the first day of school."

"It's April first now," I said. "Mom has two months to learn how to drive better."

"She'll do it, Merle. She'll be ready to go by the first of June, I bet."

"Uh-huh, she will. I won't take your bet."

As I sat back admiring the flower vases, waiting to be called to dinner, I thought about Grandmother's family. There'd been ten of them, but we'd only met three others besides her—her two sisters, Polly and Elnora, who lived in northern California, and her younger brother Varne, who lived in Oregon. One brother, Jesse, had died a long, long time back, as a young man, according to her. The others, three brothers and two sisters, lived in Oklahoma and Kansas and Missouri. I knew them only by name. They were my great-uncles Parker and Leo and Earl and my great-aunts Lucy and Beulah Land, whose name always made me want to giggle, it was so queer. They'd all be pretty old by now, though except for Earl they'd be younger than our grandmother, who was seventy-four years old. Great-aunt Elnora, who used to be a schoolteacher and who was "Miss Quiney," had come visiting us just last year. She was interesting. That was mostly because she put henna on her hair to keep it red. Grandmother didn't do that, and neither did Great-aunt Polly. She was gray-haired too, and so of course was Great-uncle

Varne, who'd been an Oregon lumberman ever since he left Texas.

Oh, there surely had been a lot of Quineys back in Santa Rosa County, in the middle of Texas! Ten was a terrible lot of kids for one family. Sometimes when I had nothing else to think about, I wondered what they did to entertain themselves when they were Graham's and my age.

The funny picture with Laurel and Hardy was good and so were the two serials. I had to admit that the one about the jungle boy, which had four more parts to be seen yet before it came to an end, was better than the beginning of *Dolores, Daughter of Doom.* I'd had high hopes for it because of the princess. Most serials, it seemed to me, had boys as the important people in them.

We didn't have to wait one minute for Dad to pick us up out front of the theater. His Essex was parked at the curb down the street, and Dad began honking the horn when we came out. He leaned over at the wheel, flung open the other door, and called out, "Crowd in, you two."

We squeezed into the little coupe, and off we went down Colorado Boulevard to our house. He looked angry. His teeth were shut hard on the stem of his pipe.

So I wisely left it to Graham to ask, "Dad, are we really going to Louisiana with Mom?"

"It seems that you are," he answered, as he cut across traffic, making a left turn with his arm stuck out the window so other drivers would know what he was doing.

"Your mother and I have had a long talk. She's going to start taking driving lessons Monday."

"Oh, but you could teach her, couldn't you, Dad?" asked my brother.

The question had been a mistake. Dad barked at him, "I will not do that. I'm not going to be party to any of this. It's your mother's idea and your grandmother's. They think they can drive coast to coast without a man along. I intend to let them learn the error of their ways. I'll pack the Studebaker with whatever you might need, kiss your mother and you two good-bye, and then shake your grandmother's hand. And then after I've sent the four of you off to New Orleans, I'll spend the summer praying for you."

"Five of us," I corrected him. "Brownie's coming too."

"Oh, yes, I'll miss her," Dad said, as he made another turn, a right one this time. "I forgot that that big, ferocious guard dog is going with you. I'll put in a heartfelt prayer now and then for her too. I'll pray that a starving coyote doesn't grab her somewhere between Arizona and New Mexico, and a panther doesn't nab her in Louisiana."

"Oh, my! Will it be that dangerous?" Graham and I asked excitedly.

"Kids, I don't know what will happen, but I'd take any bets offered that this crazy trip you're about to start on will be one you won't forget for a long time. I've traveled with your mother before you were born. She's the sort of person who has adventures. She was arrested in Spain in 1914 when we were newlyweds. She wore a bathing suit she'd bought in California on a beach there. It was the first bathing suit that this Spanish beach had ever seen. The Spanish police said it was immoral. I had to pay her way out of jail. She's never felt one bit sorry about her travel adventures. She likes to be ahead of everyone else. She was the first woman I know to bob her hair and get a radio, and *now* she's driving a car! Her friend who sold her the Studebaker was one of the first women in the country to drive a car. That woman has been a bad influence on your mother for years."

I knew the lady. She was fun, a real flapper, who wore very short skirts and rolled stockings and put rouge on her knees as well as on her cheeks. Dad thought she was a hoodoo, a bad-luck bringer. He snorted.

To calm him, I said, "But Grandmother will be along too."

"Yes, that comforts me a bit, but I have to admit that at times I have some doubts about her too. After all, she is a Quiney. There's more about that family than your grandmother has ever told any of us, I suspect. It's a big one, cousins by the dozens."

I asked, "Have you ever heard of anybody named Rudd?"

He thought for a while as he shifted gears at a stop sign. "No, I don't think I have. If he's a Quiney, he's a new one to me. Now let's forget about that family and about the ridiculous trip for a while. I'll stop at the drugstore at the next corner and get a quart of ice cream to take home. We'll make it strawberry tonight."

"That's Mom's favorite. Aren't you mad at her?" asked Graham.

"Yes, I am. But it's my favorite flavor too."

The weeks from the first of April to the first of June went fast, with Mom taking driving lessons and getting her license in the middle of May. She was a good driver, it seemed to me, when she drove all of us and Brownie down the highway to Huntington Beach in the Studebaker one Sunday. She didn't seem much fazed as she passed cars and parked and backed out of parking places. It surprised Dad that she didn't hit any other cars or anything else. She still didn't seem one bit nervous when she pulled up in front of our house.

Then she exclaimed to Dad, "Now, John, didn't I do just fine today? Are you still fretting? Am I a reckless speed hound?"

"Floy, a trip from Pasadena to the beach is not a journey of more than two thousand miles," he told her, getting out of the front seat, slamming the door, and then going up our front steps.

"He's a grouch, you know," Mom told her mother.

"So was your father, Floy."

Mom laughed, then said, "We are going to send John a postal card from every town we stay in along the way." She swiveled around in the front seat to look at me. "Merle, you can find the cards, and you can write every other one to your dad."

"But what'll I say?" I hadn't expected this sort of chore. I wasn't much for letter writing, not the way Grandmother was.

Mom giggled. "We'll write him the same thing everywhere we go. 'Having a wonderful time. Wish you were here.' That will get his goat. He'll know where we are by the postmarks on the cards. Tomorrow we're going to start packing, and as soon as you're dismissed from school, we are going bye-bye."

That was a word Graham and I had outgrown years ago, but not Brownie, who was nearly as old as Graham. She'd heard her favorite word, so did what she always did. She sat up on her hind legs and barked, waving her paws in the air. Nobody had taught her that; she'd learned it herself. Brownie was a pretty smart pooch. There was a sort of smile on her face all the time. I surely hoped she wouldn't run into coyotes or panthers anywhere. She'd have to learn how to behave in a car on a long trip. I was worried about her. I was worried about all of us.

2
The Crank

The last week, while Dad set up the Studebaker for the trip, Graham and I took turns teaching Brownie how to be a good traveler. It seems to me that every time I'd pushed the dog down in the back seat and told her "Sit," Dad came to interrupt me with some new thing he was putting into the car. The toolbox already held a lot of pliers and screwdrivers, and he'd seen to it that we had a strong towrope, an ax in case we had to hack fallen trees out of the road, a shovel in case we got stuck in the mud, four sets of tire chains, two extra tires, and a tire-repair kit.

In the meantime, Mom and Grandmother did the packing. We were all going to dress the same way on the road, in high-laced boots, khaki pants, and safari jackets, but in towns and with the Fawcetts we'd have to be more presentable so they packed everybody's better clothing in green-metal suitcases, which would be tied to the Studebaker's running boards.

Finally the morning came that we were to go. That was one to remember all right. Dad was glum as a thundercloud. We left before he went to work, so he had time for his good-byes to us. They were something to remember too. "Now you be careful, you hear me, Floy? Don't take a wrong turn anywhere. Keep the car filled with gas, and don't forget to put in oil or you'll burn out your bearings. Don't drive around curves at more than the fifteen-mile-an-hour limit. Be careful that you don't drop a drive shaft. If you notice any nuts or bolts on the ground where you've parked, get some man to put them back for you—in the right places. Fill your water bags full before you start into the desert."

Mom paused in front of the mirror in the living room to put on the wide-brimmed, tan-felt hat she wore when she drove. "Is that all, Johnny?" she asked him.

"No, it isn't, Floy. Use your tire chains in mud. Be careful of washed-out bridges. Be careful of detours. Don't let anyone overcharge you. Don't spend more than a dollar and a half for dinner or more than four dollars a night for two rooms, and make sure first that the rooms are clean. Look them over before you sleep in them." He stopped to get his breath. "I think I should have my head examined for letting you go at all. Call me long-distance wherever you are if you need me, and I'll come get you in the Essex or by train."

"We shall do that, dear, if we need rescuing." Mom put her hands on his shoulders and kissed him. He grabbed her and hugged her tight. Then he grabbed and hugged Graham and then me, calling me "honey." As he'd said, he shook Grandmother's hand and said to her, "You watch out over all of them, Susannah."

"Don't you worry about that, John." She leaned

forward and brushed her cheek against his while Brownie stood up, pawing at her boots to get her attention away from him.

After that we went down to the loaded car at the curb and waved good-bye to the neighbors who were standing out on their front lawns watching and to those who were only peeking at us from behind their curtains. We were the talk of the neighborhood because of our "boldness." Some of them thought Mom was one of the new breed of women California produced. Dad didn't come out, and we didn't see a curtain twitching either.

A friend of Graham's, a kid his age, yelled, "Ready, set, go!" as Mom started the car.

We were off.

We drove away, singing, "On the Road to Mandalay." Mom and Graham were in the front seat, Grandmother, Brownie, and I in the back with the vases. I'd put a red rose in one vase and a white one in the other.

The morning had been warm in Pasadena. As we drove through the orange groves of Riverside County it was even warmer. We perspired, though we had all of the windows down. We were around mountains now, and we had to follow a green Nash for miles through them until the Nash stopped in the town of Banning. From there on the desert began, so we got lunch, gas, and lots of water, and then drove on to the village of Palm Springs, where we stayed that night in a motor camp. While Graham and I stood outside our double cabin watching for shooting stars over the desert, Mom wrote Dad our first postcard. I already knew what it would say, of course.

That night something happened that I thought would be wise to keep to myself. Grandmother and I shared a double bed, and I found out that she talked in her sleep. She wasn't so much of a sleep talker as a sleep mumbler. I couldn't make out most of what she was saying, and she wouldn't answer questions I whispered after she'd said clear as could be, "No, sirree, Rudd, absolutely not. You go to the devil, you hear me?" She muttered something I couldn't hear very well, and then again she spoke out clearly. "You should be hit with a stick of stovewood every morning before breakfast, Rudd."

When I asked her the next morning over our breakfast waffles about any dreams she'd had, she told me that she hadn't had a single one. Well, I knew better!

All the way to Yuma, over the desert and some very bumpy roads, I thought about what she'd said, and at dinner that night I got a chance to ask Mom privately about it. "Who's Rudd? Grandmother talks to him in her sleep."

"Rudd?" Mom shook her head. "I don't know anyone by that name, Merle. Maybe he's an old boyfriend of your grandmother's."

"Then no wonder she didn't marry him if she wants to hit him with a stick," I said.

I took my mind off that after we left Yuma the next

morning. Graham and I played a game of how many cars we'd see coming the other way. The road was a fast one, with a hard surface to Gila Bend. On that busy stretch we saw two westbound cars, a Cleveland and a Franklin. From Gila Bend to Ajo there was only one, a Studebaker sort of like ours. Mom tooted our horn at it, and it tooted back.

"Isn't this fun?" she called back over her shoulder to Grandmother and me, as we left Ajo behind in our dust.

"No, I wouldn't say that it was, Floy." Grandmother was holding onto her straw hat with one hand while she kept Brownie, who was sleepy from the heat, from sliding off the back seat with her other hand. "It's hot as the hinges of Hades, and you're becoming a speed hound, dear. I can see that speedometer too. You're going over twenty-five miles an hour. We can't get a good look at the countryside unless we look back at it."

Mom laughed at her and said, "We'll make Tucson ahead of schedule. I figured on a hundred miles a day. I think I'll put it up to a hundred and fifty. Watch me. I'm going to pass that red Buick up ahead of us."

Grandmother warned, "Now, Floy, our radiator might begin to boil in this heat."

"It will boil faster if we go slower, Mother," Mom shouted over her shoulder again.

It seemed to me that she speeded all the way to Tucson, Arizona, where she slowed down because it was a town and had traffic laws.

We got a very early start away from Tucson, almost a dawn start, too early for any cafés to be open. We ate box lunches we bought the night before, sharing the food with Brownie, who seemed to like sausage and cheese, though she'd never tasted that kind of food at home.

Although the roads were oiled and fast going, it was a long way from Tucson, through the state of New Mexico, to El Paso in Texas. I thought the miles of New Mexico desert would never end, and I worried along with Grandmother about something happening to the Studebaker and our being stranded out in the middle of nowhere. But though it took us three days to cross New Mexico, nothing happened except that Graham got carsick and so did Brownie. I didn't pay much heed to the names of the towns we stopped in to buy gasoline and get fresh water and eat. I noticed, though, that while we ate Mom sent postcards to Dad from each place we stopped. I didn't send a single one, but from the way Mom grinned when she wrote them I knew exactly what she was saying on them.

By the time we reached the Texas border I was half asleep because of the heat, and I had stuck both of my bare feet out the window on my side. Graham was doing the same thing on his.

Mom's voice woke me up, and I pulled my feet in before they got more sunburned. As I straightened up, I heard her say, "Well, Mother, we'll be in El Paso in just a few minutes. How long has it been since you were here?"

"Twenty-one years as I recall, Floy, since I visited anywhere in my home state, and that was in San Antonio in 1908."

Graham asked, "Grandmother, what's El Paso like?"

"I don't know, child. It's not part of the state I know. But I've heard of it several times. I imagine it has to be large enough so we can find a nice place to stay where we can get a decent hot soak in a bathtub. I don't care one bit for shower baths."

"That suits me to a T also," Mom sang out. "I want to get the dust of the road out of my hair."

I hadn't minded shower baths in motor camps at all, but I kept quiet about that. Instead I asked, "How far away is the part of Texas where you were born, Grandmother?"

"Hundreds of miles from here, Merle. At least five hundred, I'd guess. I was born in Santa Rosa County, on a ranch, like all the rest of us Quineys."

"All ten of you," murmured my brother.

She went on. "There wasn't any town in that county large enough to talk about when we were children there, and as far as I know there still isn't."

"Is that why all of you left the ranch?" I asked.

"Yes, my oldest brother Earl sold the home place years and years ago. I imagine it's very much changed by now." She let out a sigh as she patted Brownie, who was stretched out with her head in Grandmother's lap, panting. She added after a while, "According to the route we're taking, we aren't going to pass within a hundred miles of the old home place on this trip."

I asked, "Would you like to go there again?"

"No, Merle." She looked sideways at me. "I doubt if the sight of it would gladden me much. It would make me recall some things I'd just as soon not think about." She spoke very softly, sounding sad. "We Quineys are growing old now, and we're scattered. Mama's little dozen—all gone out in the world or dead. So long ago, 1879 it was when Jesse died."

Dozen? I caught that number. Dozen meant twelve, not ten. Did she mean that there were more who'd died in 1879 than her brother, Jesse? I'd heard about him. She certainly was confusing me, so as Mom went around a corner, politely blowing the Studebaker's horn to warn anybody coming in the other direction, I said to her, "Grandmother, you just said there were a dozen of you."

"Did I, Merle?" She smiled at me. "It must be this heat that's got to me. I feel as if I'm on fire all over."

She didn't look hot to me. Brownie's tongue was lolling, and I knew I was damp all over, but I couldn't see one drop of perspiration running down the powder on Grandmother's face. Heat had never fazed her back in California either.

We saw the river Rio Grande at El Paso. It was yellow and muddy, and the hotel where we stayed overnight was also yellow, but clean enough to suit Mom and Grandmother. I got the feeling that El Paso wasn't truly Texas yet to Grandmother, because as we drove out the next morning she said it didn't seem one bit familiar to her and wasn't one bit like Santa Rosa County, as she remembered it.

It rained later that day as we drove over an uphill road to a little place called Shafter. That rain cooled us considerably, but it got us into trouble too. It made the bumps in the road slippery, and Mom worried that we might hit a bump too hard and tear off the plug in the bottom of the car's crankcase so we'd lose oil and burn out our bearings, the way Dad had feared. The road got sort of bad but exciting some miles from Shafter. Mom looked very serious and determined as we forded a creek called Antelope Creek over and over again. Graham kept count of how many times the road crossed this same little creek. It was thirteen times, and each time we worried that we'd get the Studebaker's spark plugs or battery wet so the engine would die on us, but we got through all right. Though once the creek water came up to the bottom of the running boards.

Fifty miles or so beyond the last crossing of Antelope Creek we ran into mud. It must have been raining really hard here the day before. The mud was so sticky that when Mom stepped on the gas pedal it seemed to me the Studebaker went one foot forward and three feet down. So we sat for a time, afraid to go ahead or to back up because if we did we could get in deeper.

"This is truly Texas!" Grandmother told us all. "The ground here turns to red mud when it rains."

"What'll we do, Mother?" asked Mom in a worried voice.

"I suggest that we sit here and wait until somebody comes along with a team of horses to pull us out."

After we'd been there awhile, a man came by on

horseback. He had on a big hat and boots, but the hat wasn't white or black, only brown, and the boots weren't fancy like the ones cowboys always wore in the moving pictures. His jacket was only blue cloth; there was no fringe and not one bead on it. Yet he was a real cowboy, though on first sight Graham and I didn't believe it. He was nice and polite too. He promised faithfully, when Mom asked him, to send someone to us with a team, and so he did. The team and driver arrived two hours later. The driver tied our towrope onto our front bumper and onto his team's harness, and after he yelled three times at his horses to pull hard against their collars, we were out of the mud. But not before Mom paid the driver two dollars.

"That was highway robbery, Floy!" snorted Grandmother, as we went on our way again. She poked me in the ribs but said over the seat front to Mom, "Texas has changed, Floy. When I lived here as a girl, a man wouldn't have expected a lady to pay him money for a chivalrous deed like that. He would have considered himself well paid with a smile from her."

Making conversation more than anything else, I asked, "What year did you leave Texas, Grandmother?"

"Very early in 1880. That's when I married your grandfather Fawcett, and he took me out to California as a bride."

"That was sure a long time ago," came from my brother. "How come you didn't marry somebody from Texas?"

"Graham, in those days it was not easy to find a

Texas man who was civilized enough to consider marrying!"

"But your brothers got married," I said.

"Not all of them. And some of their wives surely learned to regret their mistake." She shook her head.

Not *all* of them! I counted men Quineys in my head as the Studebaker bumped along in a light drizzle. Earl, Varne, Parker, and Leo. As far as I'd ever known, they were all married. I'd heard the names of their wives but couldn't exactly keep them straight in my head.

As Grandmother put Brownie down off her lap to lie between us, I said, "You Quineys are certainly interesting. You were half boys and half girls. What did your mother and father like best? Girls or boys?"

"Girls, I imagine, though the family did incline to boys. Your Quiney great-grandmother always used to say that her girls were easier to raise than any of those rowdy boys."

I leaned forward to tap Graham on the shoulder and say, "Did you hear that, Boy?"

"Oh, I heard her." He sounded sour, but he shouldn't have. After all, he was riding in the front seat on the right-hand side, the best place of all in a car. That was because he had a tendency to get more carsick in the back.

I lolled back against the upholstery, thinking, while I looked at the empty flower vase beside my head. Grandmother's words had set me wondering again. How could she claim that the Quineys were "inclined to boys" when the ten of them had come to five boys and five girls? I didn't want to tell her that I thought there was something wrong with her arithmetic, but it seemed to me that there surely was.

We stopped that night in a little town that was only one street long, really just a cluster of buildings on both sides of the main road. There was only one café, and all it served was beefsteak and chicken and chili beans. We stayed in a little boardinghouse that couldn't have had more than six rooms, none of them big enough to swing a cat in. The lady who ran it was particular, too, about children and pets, and Mom had to promise her that Graham and I and Brownie would behave ourselves.

Down in the parlor, just before we went to bed, Mom and Grandmother studied the map. Fort Worth, according to the map, was only sixty miles away, and some miles beyond that was Dallas. I heard Mom say, "We could make it to Dallas the next day if the roads aren't too muddy again."

The lady who ran the boardinghouse was sitting in a chair across from Grandmother, crocheting a doily. She asked where we were bound and where we'd come from and how long we'd been on the road and how did we like Texas.

When she learned that Grandmother had been born and raised in Texas, she got more friendly and wanted to know about her family.

So Grandmother talked to her about her maiden name and said that there had been ten of them born down in Santa Rosa County.

"Quiney?" said the hotel lady, making the word a question. "I do believe I used to know some Quineys when I was a girl. They were menfolks—always together they were when they came into town. I don't recall their names, but one was tall and slim and the other one small and runty. Nobody would know they were kin to one another, except that both of them had red hair—almost the same shade of red. Somewhere between orange and carrot, I'd call it." She put her crocheting down. "They were real ripsnorters, those brothers, especially that little one." She chuckled to herself. "Would they be kin of yours?"

"No, they would not," Grandmother told her. "Not close relations, if relations at all. Perhaps second or third cousins that I don't know." She handed the road map to Mom, got up, and announced, "I think it's time for all of us to go to bed, so we can get an early start in the morning."

Then the boardinghouse lady said, "I think those men were living somewhere near MacRae last I heard of them, but that was years ago."

"MacRae?" Mom looked up as she folded the map. "I remember hearing that name. Don't you get a Christmas card every year from someone from MacRae, Texas, Mother?"

"Yes, from Mrs. Hemmrich, my very dear friend of my girlhood, Carolina Hemmrich. That's where you've heard of the town." I watched her bend over, scoop Brownie up off the braided rug at her feet, and head for the stairs with the dog under her arm.

I thought that Grandmother wasn't in any mood to talk about either MacRae or her dear old friend there whom I'd never heard of. She hadn't even been very polite to the boardinghouse lady. That wasn't like her. She usually enjoyed chatting with ladies near her own age.

She got me out of bed at the crack of dawn, shaking me awake. Brownie was up on my side with her front paws on my chest. She was ready to go bye-bye.

Grandmother said, "We've got box lunches and box breakfasts, too, Merle. Hurry. Get dressed. Your mother and Graham are already down at the car."

"What's the big hurry?" I grumbled, because I hate to be wakened by anyone, even by Brownie.

"It looks like rain again. We want to get as far today as we can before the roads are so muddy again. I don't want to be stuck anywhere around these parts. Come on now. Hurry up."

Because I hurried, we were on our way in ten minutes. I hadn't even taken the time to wash my face or brush my teeth, Grandmother was in such a rush. That wasn't like her either.

"Floy, I have a premonition," she announced, as we left the one-street town behind us.

"A good one or a bad one, Mother?" Mom asked, as she looked at Grandmother in the rear-view mirror.

"You know I never have the pleasant sort. Something is going to happen. I feel it in my bones."

"Where in your bones?" asked Graham.

"My skull bones," she snapped at him. Then she said, "What I want to do is reach Dallas as soon and as safely as possible."

"I'll do my best, and I'm sure the Studebaker will too, Mother," said Mom.

We ate our box breakfast alongside the road, inside the car because it was raining. I looked past the rain at country that had been green and was turning brownish now that it was June. It was surely flat land, the flattest I had ever seen.

The landscape didn't change much as we went farther to the east. The weather changed, though, after we'd had our lunches out of some more boxes. It rained harder—so hard beyond Fort Worth that Mom complained about not being able to see the road ahead as clearly as she'd like to.

And then all at once it happened!

Mom stomped on the brakes, and the car came to a stop after skidding around on the wet road in a circle so it ended up facing the way we'd come. I let out a wild, screeching yell that should have been heard all the way home to Pasadena and Dad. Brownie was yelping on the bottom of the car, and Grandmother had her hand over her heart. In front Graham had wisely dived onto the floor while Mom was collapsed over the wheel, shaking.

"What's the matter, Floy?" Grandmother got her voice back first.

Mom lifted her head, still trembling. "It's the bridge. The bridge ahead, over the creek."

"What about it, Floy?"

"It's been washed away! I saw it only just in time to brake the car." Mom had hold of herself now, though she was white-faced, even whiter than the time Graham fell out of the swing and stunned himself. "The rain must have washed it out."

Grandmother let out a groaning sound. "It hasn't rained hard enough down here for that. It must be a flash flood—water coming down from some cloudburst north of here."

"Well, whatever it is, Mother, we can't get across here. I'll have to check the road map for a detour."

"Yes, we'll do that, of course."

So the two of them put their heads together over the map. They decided if we went back the way we'd come for a couple of miles or so, we'd find a road that ran south. We'd have to take our chances that some other bridge over that creek was still up.

But the Studebaker wouldn't start. While we sat waiting and Brownie whined, because she knew everyone was upset, Mom tried everything she'd learned in driving school and everything in the instruction book we'd brought with us. Finally she said, "It looks as if I'm going to have to crank the machine, Mother."

"Floy, I'll come out with you," said Grandmother.

"No, you'll get wet and maybe catch cold. Stay inside." And Mom was out of the car.

Grandmother said to nobody in particular, "I wish some car would come along to help us."

I told her, "We haven't seen a car for a long time, not since that old black Ford went by."

"That's true, Merle. Be careful, Floy," Grandmother called out the window. Then I heard her mutter, "I knew it. I just knew something was going to happen."

Mom didn't answer her. I looked out my side and saw her in front of the Studebaker in the rain with the big metal crank in her hands. I saw her put the crank into the car where it should go to start the engine.

"Here goes nothing, folks!" she yelled to us.

After that came a coughing roar and a jerk that threw us all forward in our seats. At the same time a scream rose up over the noises the Studebaker was making.

"What's wrong? What's happened?" Grandmother flung open the car door and went out into the rain too.

Mom was holding her right wrist in her left hand. The crank was lying on the ground at her feet. There was a look of pain on Mom's face. She cried out, "It was the crank. I think maybe I've broken my wrist. The cranking did it."

"Oh, my Lord!" Grandmother looked up into the dripping sky as if she was going to tell it to quit. Then she asked Mom, "The nearest place to here is MacRae, isn't it?"

"Yes, it is," said Mom weakly, still holding her wrist. The heavy steel crank must have hit hard when the engine caught. Yet even if she'd hurt herself, she had started the Studebaker. The engine was running now.

Grandmother nodded slowly and said a very strange

thing. "It's the hand of fate, all right. I should have known it would catch up with me in Texas. So I'm going to have to see both of them again!"

"What do you mean, Mother?" Mom sounded irritated. Grandmother was being very dramatic.

"I mean your Quiney uncles whose names you have never heard because they have not crossed my lips in forty-eight years."

"Who? What uncles?"

"Rudd and Hoyt. They live in MacRae. Mrs. Hemmrich keeps house for them. She said in her last Christmas card that they were still alive and kicking."

Rudd? I caught the name I'd heard before and the name of Hoyt too. So there had really been twelve Quineys! And if they lived in MacRae, we were close to them at this moment.

"I take it you mean we ought to go to MacRae now, Mother?" Mom said. "How are we going to get there? I can't drive. Not in this weather and with this bad wrist."

"No, you cannot. *I* shall have to drive!" said Grandmother grimly—but calmly. "Floy, you sit beside me and tell me what to do." She called back to my brother, "Graham, get out and get into the back seat with Merle. You two keep Brownie under control back there."

I cried to her, "What else can we do to help out?"

"You could both of you pray. Pray that we get to MacRae all in one piece, and out of it the same way."

3
The Strays

While Graham and I held our breaths and Mom gave out a steady stream of orders, Grandmother took over the wheel of the Studebaker. First Mom released the hand brake of the car with her uninjured hand. Then she said, "Now, Mother, be careful. I'll do the shifting of the gears for you. First, though, I'll tell you when to step on the clutch pedal. Steer right ahead of you, and pretend to yourself that there's a line down the middle of the road, even if there isn't any. Stay on the right side of it."

Grandmother told her almost angrily, "Floy, I know that from watching you all this time. Why don't you tell me to pretend that the road's paved while I'm at it? You keep your eye peeled for road signs that tell us where to detour, and just you let me do the rest."

Somehow we got started after a couple of teeth-rattling jerks and moved off down the road. Then the car hit a muddy stretch and skidded across the road, but Grandmother got the wheel under control before we went down into the ditch on the left side. "There, see, I can do it! Though it's a bit like waltzing on a just-waxed floor. Don't you worry. I'll have the hang of it in a minute. If only it wouldn't buck about so. I only hope I don't meet another car, and he skids right while I'm skidding left."

"Do you want us to keep on praying, Grandma?" asked Graham over the engine's coughing.

Mom answered him. "Yes, don't you stop for a minute. You too, Merle."

I sat in the back seat with Brownie in my arms, mostly thinking and only now and then praying hard, when the car skidded more than usual or looked about to be mired in mud again. I was wondering about Rudd and Hoyt, the two Quineys who had popped up out of nowhere. From the way Mom had asked "Who?" she didn't know about them either. Why hadn't she heard about them? They were her uncles, of course. Why were they a secret Grandmother had kept to herself? Why did Grandmother keep them out of the head count of her family? Were they older than she was or younger? I thought back to the people in her family I'd met in California. Not one of them had mentioned a Rudd or a Hoyt, but then I hadn't been within earshot all the time they were talking with Grandmother.

Because she seemed to be doing quite well with the Studebaker now that she was on a straight stretch of road, I decided it would be nice of me to take her mind off her troubles. "Grandmother," I said, "I never heard you talk about the uncles in MacRae until just now."

"That's right, you didn't. I never discuss the pair of them."

Graham must have been thinking, too. All at once he asked, "Why not? Are they bank robbers?"

"Certainly not. There have never been any criminals among the Quineys."

She started to turn her head to glare at Graham, but Mom warned her quickly, "Mother, keep your eyes on the road. The turnoff to MacRae has to come up at any moment now. We can't afford to miss it. I don't want you to have to make a U-turn no matter what."

"All right, Floy, but Rudd and Hoyt are not criminals."

"Oh." Graham sounded disappointed.

I'd had another idea. "Are they crazy, maybe?" I asked.

"No." Grandmother even laughed. "But Mrs. Hemmrich claims she's going crazy, and they're the cause of it."

I thought now I understood why Grandmother had seemed rude to the boardinghouse lady last night. The two Quiney men that lady had been talking about were my great-uncles. They were close kin after all. One was tall, the other runty, but both had orange-red hair. She'd said something else too—that they had been ripsnorters. I thought I knew what that meant, though it wasn't an expression I'd often heard used in Pasadena. It meant wild.

But then the boardinghouse lady had been near Grandmother's age, and she'd said she knew the Quineys when she was a girl. That would have been a long time ago—probably fifty years or more. That was a whole half a century ago.

I started to ask exactly what a ripsnorter was, but just then Mom pointed past Grandmother's nose and said, "Look, there's a sign that says MacRae—one mile. Slow down a minute, so I can read the population number on the sign."

I peered at the sign, too, through the rain. It read: *MacRae Pop. 22.*

Mom said, "Oh Lord, Mother, we might drive right through it on the detour if it's only got twenty-two people."

"No, Floy, we won't miss it. It has five houses and a cotton gin. We'll keep looking for the cotton gin. Mrs. Hemmrich wrote me about that. It should be the biggest thing in town. Now, Floy, how do I make a turn off this road?"

"Grab the wheel firmly, and turn it just a little bit to the right. Easy does it, Mother. Whatever you do, don't let the engine die. Wait till you see the arrow that points to the turnoff. I'm going to shift gears for you now. Step on the clutch pedal first, then let it out slowly after I've shifted for you." A second later she said, "Now, Mother, start your turn."

Grandmother cried, "All right, Floy. Here goes. Everybody hang on tight. We're changing directions."

I closed my eyes rather than watch her move the wheel, but I could feel the car slithering into a fast right turn that threw Brownie and me over onto Graham, who cried out as he banged his head into the flower vase on his side.

A minute later Grandmother asked Mom, "How's your wrist, Floy? I'm sorry you banged it on the car door just now."

"It hurts like the devil, Mother. I hope it isn't broken."

"Well, don't you worry. I've made that dangerous turn successfully in spite of this bucking machine. Carolina knows something about broken bones and burns and things like that. She'll get a doctor for you if it's broken. She'll understand our situation." Grandmother moaned as the Studebaker slid toward the left again in the mud, and she had to coax it back to the right lane. "If there's any one thing that could ruin this trip for me," she said, "it would be the prospect of a very long visit with my little brothers."

Little brothers? Then they were younger than she was. I wondered by how much. She answered my question before I got it out. "First comes my brother Earl, then me, then Rudd, then Varne, then Hoyt, and after that the others come trailing in. Rudd's the one who always used to lick the spout of the syrup jug after he had poured syrup on his flannel cakes. No one could ever break him of the habit, though just about everybody tried—except, of course, for Hoyt." She sighed. "I wonder if poor dear Carolina has had any luck with him."

"He licked the spout of the syrup?" Mom sounded shocked. "When did you see Uncle Rudd last?" she asked.

"In 1881. I remember the year distinctly and all that went on. How could I ever forget it? And don't you ask me about it, please. My blood still boils when I think about the last time I saw him. Telling you now would only make me more nervous than I am at the moment, and I need to remain calm if I am to drive this thing."

Graham was interested in what she'd said about the syrup jug too. He asked the question that was on the tip of my tongue. "Did Great-uncle Hoyt lick the spout of the syrup jug too?"

"I don't remember for sure, but Hoyt was always inclined as a boy to do what Rudd did. People used to remark on it. You might say that Rudd sometimes set Hoyt a bad example."

My brother said, "Gosh, they must have been something if you haven't looked them up since 1881!"

"They were, indeed, Graham. It isn't Hoyt I've avoided seeing. It's Rudd, and Hoyt is always with him."

We were in MacRae just a minute or so later. If we'd all sneezed and she'd kept on driving, we would have missed it completely. One sign only let us know where we were. It was a badly lettered one on the side of a filling station that said, *MacRae, Texas. Get Your Kerosene and Gas Here. Dirt Cheap.*

"At least, the town has something else to it besides a cotton gin," Mom told Grandmother. "We can fill up our tank here before we leave. Do you happen to know from Mrs. Hemmrich's Christmas card which house belongs to your brothers? I don't think the place is so large that it has any need of street numbers or street names."

"Floy, they live two doors from the cotton gin. I know that the house has a veranda and picket fence and that there's a rose and herb garden. Carolina has to have her garden wherever she lives—even on the reservation—no matter what trouble it brings her. She's written that she had to cope with Quiney goats here as well as insects."

"Goats?" Mother asked feebly.

"Yes. At one time, according to a Christmas-card message, Hoyt and Rudd were briefly in the goat-milk business, but they gave it up."

Grandmother leaned forward to peer through the muddy windshield at the road ahead. She nodded. "That's got to be the house, the one on the left-hand side of the road. The all-white one. It's two doors away from the cotton gin, that big wooden building. Yes, the house has a picket fence, like she said." Now her voice rose. "Floy, how do you stop this confounded machine?"

"Put your foot on the clutch pedal the way you did before while I shift into neutral. Then take your right foot off the gas, and put it on the brake pedal. Then twist the wheel just a little teeny bit to the left, and let the car cross the road to park. Next, you turn the engine off by turning the key in the ignition switch. Finally, you pull up the hand brake and get out of the car."

"That sounds simple enough. It leaves me about five things to do all at once, it seems to me. Here we go. Brace yourself everyone. Hold Brownie tight."

Once more I closed my eyes. I felt the car jerk twice, then slide over the road. Now I heard the interesting sound, a small crunching one. Either Grandmother and Mother hadn't done everything right, or they hadn't done the right things at the right time. The Studebaker had plowed into a post that held a mailbox on its top and had gone past the post a ways until Mom had reached over and with her good hand turned off the engine and hauled up the hand brake.

Yes, the mailbox was still nailed to the post, but it was leaning on the front fender on my side of the car. I was close enough to read the letters painted on the box. They said, *Quiney, H., Quiney, R., Hemmrich, C., (Mrs.).*

I exclaimed, "We're here, Grandma. We've hit the right place."

She wasn't paying any heed to me, though. She was looking into the rear-view mirror, not at the road behind her, but at her own face while she fussed with her hair and her hat. She said, "I do wish now I'd let that silly little girl at the beauty parlor put some henna on my hair. The last time Rudd set eyes on me I was a strawberry blonde. Oh, well, that's fate again. I have to appear in front of him at my worst."

She pressed her palm on the Studebaker's horn, something that didn't seem necessary to me because two people were already coming out onto the veranda. I figured the crashing sound of the mailbox post had attracted them.

One of the pair was a little, gray-haired woman in a long, pink apron. The other was a man not much bigger than she was, wearing a big hat and a green-and-black checkered shirt. He was little bit bowlegged.

"Oh, yes, that's Rudd," Grandmother announced in a flat voice. "And that's Carolina with him. Please let me do the talking." She'd folded her arms across her chest, and she wasn't smiling.

I looked away from her to the people, who were still on the veranda, nodding at one another and gesturing with their hands. The old man raised his fist and shook it at the car, then came swinging down the pathway toward the gate in the picket fence.

"That's certainly Rudd," said Grandmother again. "The best thing to do is for me to meet him head on." She got out of the car, stood beside it, and called out, "Rudd Quiney, isn't it?"

He paused on the path and waited until Mrs. Hemmrich caught up with him. The woman came running forward, past him, crying out, "Oh, Susannah! Oh my Lord be praised, it *is* you."

I opened my car window some more to hear what they were saying. Grandmother went forward with her arms outstretched. The two old ladies embraced over the gate, which couldn't have been a very comfortable thing to do, but it didn't seem to bother them. I kept my eyes on my mysterious newly discovered great-uncle. He stood watching while the women hugged. Then I saw him tilt back his hat and stare at Grandmother. Walking carefully, he came closer to her, still staring.

Then I heard him hoot in a high voice, "Billy bedamned, if it ain't her herself, my sister! Little old Brown-eyed Susie! How are you, y'old pike?" He didn't embrace her. He slapped her on the back.

Grandmother drew away from her lady friend now, looked a long moment at her brother, and said every bit as loudly as he had, "How are you, you old fence-cutting wind belly of a longhorn?"

He bent double, slapping his knees with both hands, then laughed and shouted at her, "You ain't changed so much that I wouldn't know you except that you ain't redheaded no more, and you're carryin' a lot more tallow than you used to."

Grandmother lifted her voice higher than I'd ever heard it. "Yes, Rudd, you barnyard savage. I've got gray hair, but I notice yours is white, and yes, I've put on some weight. It seems to me, though, that you're still skinny enough to split a hailstone. You were always too mean-natured for food to stick to your bones."

Mrs. Hemmrich had a soft, sweet voice, but it carried enough for me to hear too. It seemed to me all three of them meant to be heard. "Now, Rudd, your big sister has come hundreds of miles, and you haven't seen her in a long, long time. Be pleasant now."

He said, "Yep, it's long gone by since we set eyes on each other. Don't try to tell me she come a-visitin' because she was pinin' to see old Hoyt and me. Somethin' else brung her here. What're you doin' here, Sue?"

"You are correct, Rudd. I haven't come dropping in just for a visit. There's been an accident with the car. I came here to ask for Carolina's help—not for yours."

He pointed at the Studebaker. "I knowed that had to be it. A accident? With that confounded contraption, huh? You hit my mailbox, didn't you? That's what comes of not stickin' with horses! No self-respectin' horse ever hit a mailbox. You was drivin' through

MacRae on your way to somewheres else, and you hit my mailbox outa spite, and that made you stop."

I watched Grandmother's chest grow bigger as she took in a very deep breath. "No, Rudd, that isn't it at all. It's my daughter, Floy. She hurt her wrist some miles away from here where a bridge washed out."

"You don't say? Well now. . . ." His voice got lower all at once as he talked to Grandmother and Mrs. Hemmrich. Then he set his hat back squarely on his head.

"Great heavens, kids," Mom said. "I never dreamed your grandmother could talk like that. I never heard such language before from her. But he seems to understand it. Do you suppose that's how the Quineys used to talk among themselves when they were children?"

"I sure hope so," my brother said. "It isn't one bit like Pasadena talk. It sounds a little bit like cowboy talk in the moving pictures."

"Thank the Lord no one in Pasadena talks like that. Now you be on your best behavior, Graham. Here they come now."

Brownie had got loose sometime back and had walked over me to put her paws up below the window and stick her head out in the rain. She didn't like having Grandmother out of her sight for so long. When she spotted the three of them coming through the gate, she let out a yelp to let Grandmother know she'd seen her.

I heard Great-uncle Rudd saying, "That's a funny kinda voice your gal's got, Sue."

"Don't be ridiculous, Rudd. That's my dog."

Because the windshield and windows were so spattered with red mud, they couldn't see inside at all. I started to grab Brownie and go out to meet the old people, but Great-uncle Rudd got to the car before I could get out. He jerked the back door open on my side and stuck his head inside. At that instant Brownie made a dive for him. I hauled her back just in time.

I looked up while Rudd Quiney looked down, grinning at Brownie, Graham, and me. He didn't resemble Grandmother much. His eyes were light blue and crinkly at the corners in a face wrinkled and a sort of pecan-brown color from all the time he'd been out in the sun. His nose was broader and shorter than hers, and his hair under his hat was curling and white as could be. But, oh my, below his hat—he was truly different! On both sides of his head were copper-colored sideburns. The bottom part of his right ear looked like any ear I'd seen. *But the bottom part of his left ear wasn't there at all!*

I heard Graham gasping and knew he'd noticed it too, but like me he was too polite to point.

"Howdy," was our Great-uncle Rudd's first word to the two of us. Then he looked over the seat at Mom and said, "You'd be Floy, wouldn't you? You got Quiney hair, and you're Quiney handsome too. Pretty as a red-painted wagon in a medicine show. Is these here two brown-haired colts your two?" He pointed at us.

"Yes, they are." Mom's voice sounded weak, I thought.

He stared at us again and then at Brownie, who was growling at him by now. He said, "I got to say Miss Floy that your ma, my sister, is the most set-in-her-ways female I ever knowed. I hope you don't take after her. What's the name of your young uns?"

"My daughter's named Merle and my son, Graham. I'm Mrs. John Tucker." Mom gave him a sort of smile, then added, "The dog's called Brownie."

"That ain't a dog. It's a earwig, given the size of it. Merle ain't much of a handle for a gal, but how come you gave a boy a front handle like Graham? I bet everybody at his school calls him Graham Cracker because of that. I bet he hates it too."

Once more I heard my brother gasp. Then he said, "How did you know? That is what they call me, and I do hate it."

"Sure, you hate it. I'm gonna call you Tuck after a *honcho* I had a long time ago, and I'll call your sister, Missy. I hope that'll set right with you, Tuck."

"Rudd, that's enough." This was Mrs. Hemmrich's voice from behind him.

"Not quite enough, Carolina." He looked at Mom again while I held Brownie struggling against me. "How's your wing, lady? Is it mebbe busted? You're welcome to stay here long as you want to if you can stand Carolina's cookin' and her preachin' at me and Hoyt. I'll try to tolerate that pike of a ma of yours, my sister Sue. If you're in need of a doctor, Hoyt or me'll mebbe saddle up even if it ain't good for the horse and ride to Fort Worth after one. And if your wrist ain't busted, Carolina can fix you up jest dandy—long as the signs a heaven aren't up against it."

I heard Mom giggling. Then she said, "Thank you for your offer of hospitality, Uncle Rudd, but before we accept it, please tell me what pike means."

"A cow with warts. That's what I always called your ma when we was young together down in Santa Rosa County."

"Rudd!" This was Mrs. Hemmrich again. "Please, Rudd, go back to the house and wake your brother up and tell him to put the coffeepot on the front of the stove because we have company."

"Aw right, Carolina." He backed out and away so she could take his place looking into the car. She had a sweet smile and a nice face with gentle blue eyes. She told all of us, "You're mighty welcome here. Don't pay much heed to him. I've heard all about you from your grandmother's letters. She used to be the prettiest girl in Santa Rosa County—no matter what he called her. I'll see to your arm right off, Floy. I've done some nursing on the reservation in my time. You come on in now. Don't let Rudd faze you no matter what he says. For all the crowing he does, he's a chicken-hearted old rooster in my estimation."

And she started back toward the house, too, but not before Graham asked, "How did he lose part of his left ear?"

Mrs. Hemmrich sighed. "I think you'd best ask him that yourself."

"Won't it embarrass him?" I asked.

"No, I doubt that it will. It never has before. Go right ahead and ask him." And she was gone.

As I got up, tucking Brownie under my arm, I asked Grandmother, who was opening the front door to help Mom out, "Where did you ever learn to talk like that?"

"That's the way we all talked once, Merle. It's cowboy talk."

Graham sounded admiring as he asked, "Gosh, are there a lot of men in Texas like Great-uncle Rudd?"

She told him in a dry-as-a-bone voice, "They don't make men like Rudd Quiney anymore."

"He's going to call me Tuck," my brother said, as he got out behind me. "Did you ever hear that name before?"

"It's a cowboy name. It doesn't just come from your name being Tucker."

"A cowboy name! Was he ever a real cowboy?"

"Yes, he was."

"A real one?"

She nodded, smiling a little. "Yes, a real one. At one time or another all of my brothers were. In time, most of them got over it, though."

Mom asked Grandmother, "Do you think it will be all right for us to stay here for a while? Mrs. Hemmrich seems all right, but I just don't know about Uncle Rudd."

"I tell you that it's fate, Floy. I believe now that I was destined to come here all along. As for you and the children, look upon our stay here as another of your adventures while traveling." Grandmother stood in the rain that had turned into just a drizzle now, watching her brother and her friend go up onto the veranda. There was a look on her face I couldn't figure out at all. It seemed to me to be half amusement, half sadness. She shook her head and told us, "I wouldn't have thought I'd remember the way I talked as a young person, but the minute I saw Rudd again, it came back to me. You know, there's an old Texas saying that fits my situation with him every time I see him. It says 'Anybody can walk safe over quicksand as long as he don't stop for a second. If he stops, he sinks down in it.' "

"What does that mean?" Graham asked.

"It means to take every minute around Rudd as it comes. Don't get angry no matter what. Take your hints on how to behave from Carolina and me. She's kept house for him and Hoyt for years. After Reverend Hemmrich died, she had no family of her own left."

Mom was looking at her wrist and hand now. They were swelling up, turning puffy and sort of red, and looked as if they hurt. She said to Grandmother, "I didn't know your friend was a minister's wife."

"Yes, indeed, Floy. It would require a preacher's widow to keep house for Rudd and Hoyt. The woman who can do that needs a good name as a cook, the patience of a tortoise, the endurance of a buffalo, the firmness of purpose of a coyote trying to steal a chicken from a coop, and the saintly nature of a person not born in this state. Carolina has all of these qualities. She was born in New York."

"Good gracious." Mom took her worried gaze from her wrist. "What's she doing all the way out here?"

"She came west with her husband when he traveled to Texas to minister to the Comanche Indians. I know that Carolina enjoyed life among the Comanches on their reservation. Now we'd better go inside before Hoyt comes out, too."

Behind the fence some of Mrs. Hemmrich's roses were in bloom, pink and red, but mostly yellow ones. I looked at them as I went by with Brownie. They weren't as big as Mom's Pasadena roses, but they were very bright colored.

There were three chairs on the veranda. One was a plain old rocker; the other two were the strangest things I'd ever seen. They were yellow, and they stuck out in all directions around the red pillow set in the middle of each one.

Grandmother must have read my mind, for she said, "I see that our best chairs are here. Hoyt must have won them in a poker game from Earl."

"Mother, what on earth are they made out of?"

"Horns, Floy. The horns of longhorn steers. I imagine that they're museum pieces by now."

"Grandmother, what does that mean?" I knew what a museum was, but not what a museum piece was.

Mom explained, "It means that a museum would put them in collections of furniture if they had them."

Grandmother added, "They don't make them like that in Texas anymore."

"Like Great-uncle Rudd, you mean?"

She turned her head at the door, chuckling. "Yes, but the only way they'd ever accept him would be stuffed."

I think she might have said something more that was funny except the door opened all at once and a man was standing there. He was very tall and leaning on a cane. He had to be Hoyt Quiney. I thought he looked more like Grandmother than Rudd had. He was grinning. "I'd be Hoyt. Come on in, Susie. Rudd told me you and your family was here. You can see that I'm stove up, but I'm surely glad to see you, bedamned if I ain't. Come on in, I say. The queen of the pots is busy stirring up the fire. Come in, and stay as long as you want to or need to."

"Hoyt!" cried Grandmother. "Oh, Hoyt, dear."

We all stood back, waiting, as she went in first to hug her brother.

He told her as he hugged her with his free arm, "You ain't changed a bit. You're still prettier than a heifer in a bed a daisies."

She said against his shoulder, her head away from us, "You always were a flannel-mouth liar, Hoyt. I know I walk like a sore-footed steer these days, and I'm older than the hills."

"Hush," he told her. "You hush up, Brown-eyed Susie. Why have you been gone so long? It's long gone by since Rudd and I seen you. But you always kept in touch with me through Carolina, didn't you?"

"Oh, Hoyt, I always did."

"We knowed that, Rudd and me. We two strays would a writ somethin' on all them cards she sent you at Christmas if we coulda wrote."

"Oh, stop it, Hoyt. I understand. We're here only as long as need be for Floy to be able to drive again. We don't want to be bothers to you. I wasn't at all sure we'd be welcome after what happened with Rudd."

"Sue, you won't be no trouble to us at all. Glad to have you, long as you want to stay. Carolina and me together, we can maybe take care of Rudd. Two against one, remember? It always worked before in the family. We'll handle the old red rooster."

I spoke very softly to Mom so neither Grandmother nor Great-uncle Hoyt would hear me. "It's odd. I can't tell if she loves her brothers or hates them."

"Sh-h-h." Mom squeezed my shoulder with her good hand. She was smiling. "I hear that's the way it sometimes is in the best of families."

4

We Fought like Fiends!

The inside of the white house wasn't anywhere near as interesting as the horn chairs. It was just plain old-fashioned, that's all, with yellow-oak furniture, red-and-green, velvet-upholstered chairs that were faded, a rose-patterned rug, and an organ. There wasn't a radio to be seen. At home in Pasadena we had the latest style—bead curtains between rooms and fringed Spanish shawls on the piano and Tiffany lamps. This house didn't smell of incense either but of dried rose leaves and of something else—tobacco. Great-uncle Hoyt smoked cigars while Great-uncle Rudd not only smoked cigars, he chewed tobacco. There was a big brass cuspidor in the living room for him and another in the kitchen, and I guessed there must be one in his bedroom too.

Our great-uncles and Graham and I sat down in the parlor. Mom and Grandmother, who'd taken Brownie from me, went out to the kitchen when Mrs. Hemmrich called to them, "You girls come on out here, please, so I can have a look at that wrist of Floy's."

We could hear some murmurings from out there and the clankings of pots and pans, along with some nice smells, that let us know food was being cooked. It was only about three o'clock, but it seemed to me to have been a long time since my box lunch, and a lot had certainly happened since then, not to mention that we'd found two missing Quineys!

Pretty soon Mom came out, leaving Grandmother in the kitchen. Mom's wrist looked worse now, turning reddish violet. She said, "Mrs. Hemmrich says it's a very bad sprain and that it would be dangerous for me to drive for at least five days. She sent me out to tell you. Then I have to go back to the kitchen and soak my wrist."

Great-uncle Hoyt was in a rocking chair, rocking. "Then you'll be stayin' here with us for that long," he said, sounding quite pleased. "Won't that be nice, Rudd?"

Great-uncle Rudd was rocking in his chair near the organ and cuspidor. He had his hat still on the back of his head. Hoyt was bareheaded. "I dunno, Hoyt," he said. "It all depends on little old Sue and on how much she gets in my way. I like things done my way here."

Mom asked Great-uncle Hoyt, not even looking at Rudd, "Is there any hotel closer than Dallas or Fort Worth?"

"Nope, Floy, there ain't."

"Well," said Mom, biting her lower lip as if she was thinking hard, "could one of you drive us to either city, so we could put up there? We don't want to be a bother to you."

Rudd told her, "Nobody here can drive a stink carriage, which is what I call automobiles. We ain't speed demons like some folks I could mention but won't. The horse is still plenty good enough for us." Oh, but he could be rude!

Mom looked directly at him, and I thought she was angrier than she let on. I know that I would have been. "All right then," she said. "Could you take us to town in a buggy? Then, when I can drive, I could return and get the car."

"We ain't got no more horses except for one, and we ain't had a buggy since last month when it broke down for good and I had to shoot it." Then Great-uncle Rudd tilted his hat to one side, staring at Graham and me to see if we had liked his joke.

Neither Graham nor I even smiled. I was proud of my brother for that.

Rudd Quiney went on. "I was only funnin' you, you pair of sprouts. Hoyt's got the right of it. Sure, you can bunk down here. We got some space and lotsa grub. I'd take it very unkindly if you was to go anyplace else." He reached into his pocket, pulled out a plug of tobacco, bit off a chunk of it, and stuffed it into his mouth to chew. He looked up at Mom. "You hear me? You're stayin' here with us long as you need to, little lady."

"Yes, Uncle Rudd. Thank you." Mom turned around, holding her wrist, and went off toward the back of the house. I was proud of her for not telling him what she thought of his manners. Rude Quiney was what he should have been named.

I said to the two old men, "Her wrist hurts her a lot." I got up from the sofa where I was sitting with Graham. "I think I'll go out and see how she's doing."

"No cause for you to do that, Missy," said Great-uncle Rudd. "She'll be doin' jest fine. Carolina's a good hand with doctorin'. The kitchen is plumb full of females, and they don't need no more out there."

Suddenly he lifted his left hand to the side of his head, cupping it behind the two thirds of an ear he still had there. "Missy," he asked, "ain't you two at all interested in how I come to lose this piece of myself?"

I was too shocked to say anything, but not Graham. "Sure we are, if you want to tell us. But Mom would be mad at us if either of us came right out and asked you. She was really mad at me when I asked the boy up the street about how he got his shoes on when he had six toes."

Great-uncle Rudd nodded while Great-uncle Hoyt looked at the ceiling and rocked. He'd set his cane down on the rug beside him.

"How did the boy get into his shoes, Tuck?" Rudd wanted to know.

"He sticks one toe under another toe."

"Ah?" came from the old man. "That's how he does it! I take it you're speakin' for your sister, too? You want to hear how I lost part of this old ear of mine then? Well, as you may have guessed, I wasn't born with a part of an ear missin'. I came by that very unnaturally."

"Yes, indeed you did," Great-uncle Hoyt said quietly.

He looked up from his rocker at me. "You'd best sit down. This could take quite a while."

"You bet," Great-uncle Rudd told us. "Supper won't be on the table till five o'clock, the time me and Hoyt like it to be ready. So y'all have got the time to hear what I'm gonna tell you."

I sat down on the sofa again, trying not to stare at the peculiar ear. I could tell Graham was doing the same thing because of the way he was staring at the carpet, which wasn't one bit interesting.

"We always fought like fiends," Great-uncle Rudd began.

Graham asked, "You and Grandma?"

"No, Tuck, I'm not referrin' to her. I'm tellin' this story, and I don't take kindly to bein' interrupted by anybody. I'm talkin' about us Texans back during the war. And I don't mean the war we fought against Spain back in 1898. I mean the big important one further back—the Civil War. That's the one I lost part of my ear in. Billy bedamned, if I didn't. That time is long gone by, but I remember it like it was yesterday."

He took a deep breath to begin, but just then Brownie let out a small yip in the kitchen. "That's a mouthy dog you brung with you, ain't it, Tuck? Is it a him or a her dog?"

"A her dog. I mean Brownie's a female. She isn't our dog. She's Grandma's dog."

"I mighta knowed it'd be her pooch by the earwig size of it and its yappiness. I hope it ain't gonna give us no trouble here and interfere with our sleepin' nights, or I'll pitch it into a deep gully I know nearby."

I put in quickly, "Brownie's never a bit of trouble to anyone. All Grandmother has to say to her is 'Hush,' and she stops barking." I don't know why, but Great-uncle Hoyt chuckled and turned toward his brother.

Rudd gave him a funny look, then looked back at Graham and me. "As I was sayin', us Texas men was fiendish fighters. Our leader was a giant of a man by the name of General John B. Hood. He was born in Kentucky, but us Texans forgave him for it because he was such a dandy soldier and a great favorite of General Robert E. Lee."

"I heard of Lee at school last year," said Graham. "I wrote a book report on his life."

"Sure, you know about him, Tuck. Everybody knows about Lee. As I was sayin', Hood come over to the Confederate side back in 1861. He gave up a commission in the U. S. Army to do that and join up with the Confederate side. In May of 1861 he was a lieutenant, but by that September he was a colonel. It was in Richmond, Virginia, which was the capital of the Confederacy, that old Hood met me first."

"Were you a colonel, too?" asked Graham.

"No, I wasn't. I wasn't no more than twenty years old then."

"Yep, Rudd, some folks might say that you was sort of young then," said Great-uncle Hoyt.

"I was a young snort, I grant you that, but even at

that age I knowed my oats. Naturally, here in Texas we'd gotten the news that there was a Civil War goin' on. So some of us brave lads from Santa Rosa County got together, and we decided it would be very kindly of us to help out the Confederacy. So takin' six weeks to get around to every one of 'em, we kissed the purty gals for miles around farewell, got on our horses, and rode toward the risin' sun as the Texas Volunteers."

"Rudd rode east," said Great-uncle Hoyt.

"That's right. That's the very direction we took to Virginia, where a Texas Brigade was bein' put together under General Hood. Me and my old friend Clee Puttiphut joined the Texas Brigade together. Clee's pa owned the horse ranch ten miles up the road from the Quiney spread. The Puttiphut cattle brand was the old flyin' V."

"Keep to the Civil War, Rudd," said Hoyt Quiney.

"I surely will. General Hood was right away pleased to find us Texans the most fiendish fighters in the Confederacy. We first went into action under him in May, 1862. Everywhere me and Clee and General Hood came, them Yankees wisely ran away to keep out of our reach. They knew us by reputation, of course, as Texans, and they knew our leader. Good old General Hood walked right along with us into them enemy guns in Virginia, and it ain't at all a common thing for generals to do any walking."

"Weren't you riding on horses? Weren't you cowboys?" asked Graham, who sounded upset. I thought it was odd too.

"Sure, we was mostly all of us cowboys, but sometimes we cowboys walked in the Civil War. Not that Texans ever *favored* walkin', you understand, Tuck. It was only because of the war."

"Oh!" said my brother breathing hard as he stared at the old man. He'd finally met a real true cowboy, not one in moving pictures. Oh, he was thrilled!

Great-uncle Rudd stopped to spit tobacco juice into the cuspidor. Then he went on. "To get on with how I lost part of my ear. I lost it in the state of Maryland. The sad event took place in the year 1862, in September. It was near a town the Confederates called Sharpsburg, and it seems to me the Yankees called it Antietam. There was a battle there. In later years me and Clee Puttiphut claimed to each other we'd never forget it—it was so fierce. It was a battle where we truly fought like fiends. Sharpsburg is where the damnyankees proved to us that they could cut the mustard as soldiers when they'd a mind to. They didn't run from us Confederates there. General Robert E. Lee, the head Confederate general of them all, was there at Sharpsburg along with Clee and me and General Hood. It was Lee's desire to hit them Yankees hard as he could. He would have liked to end the Civil War right then and there. War wasn't a thing he took much pleasure in."

"Was General Ulysses S. Grant there, too?" asked Graham. "I wrote a book report on Grant's life, too, but I can't remember anymore where he was fighting from month to month."

"Tuck, don't you never mention his Yankee name in

this house again. I'll forgive you now, because it's the first time you said it. Grant wasn't there as I recall it. He was elsewhere."

"All right, I won't mention him ever again." My brother surely was taking to his new name. I thought I could see why. It was better than Graham and a lot better than Missy. I certainly didn't much like that for myself, but right now I didn't say so. Later on, when I knew my great-uncles better, I'd let them know that I wanted it changed. Now, however, I thought I'd better say something to let them know I was there, listening too—not just Graham.

So I said, "I promise not to mention General Grant's name either. Please go on with your story."

Great-uncle Rudd gave me a nod. "Well, sir, it was General Lee's bold plan to end the war on Northern soil and by doin' that give the Yankees a taste of their own medicine. So Lee and his Confederates made a stand in Maryland. The spot Lee picked was at Sharpsburg, which is close to a creek called Antietam Creek, which must be why the Yankees call the battle the Battle of Antietam.

"Me and Clee Puttiphut came there to Sharpsburg along with our General Hood, because Lee was collectin' generals to help him whip the Yankees. Generals like to have lots more generals around to comfort 'em, I suppose. But Lee had other men too. Cavalry—horse soldiers—and some foot soldiers and some cannons. General Lee put his men behind some steep banks along that piddling Antietam Creek as well as in some other places."

Great-uncle Rudd looked up at a twisting crack in the ceiling for a moment, shook his head, and let out a sigh before he went on. "Sometimes armies get lost in strange country. It'd be hard to lose a whole army in Texas, which is far-famed for its flatness. But in the East it now and then happened because of all them woods and hills. An army is always on the lookout for the enemy army, as you can probably figger out for yourself. That's the way it has to be with armies."

"I can see that," put in my brother.

"Yes, sir," Great-uncle Hoyt said. "Go on with the story, Rudd."

"Well, sir, them damnyankees come down a road in the night, bein' very wary of General Lee wherever he might be. The Yankees were aimin' to join up with some other Yankee troops, but instead they ran smack-dab into us Confederates. What they saw when dawn came that rainy day was a little white church in a grove of trees and on its left a field of corn tall as a tall man. And what did they see all around the little church but us Confederates! One of our best generals was there at the church with his cannons and his infantry. The cornfield was jest full of infantry—foot soldiers—and in a pasture on the right of the church was another good general of Lee's with his cavalry. That part of Maryland was plumb full of gray-coated men. Mosta us Confederates wore gray, you see."

Hoyt explained, "The Yankees wore blue coats so the armies could be told apart. That was important—that they be told apart." He was grinning and nodding at Rudd.

"Yep, we called 'em blue bellies sometimes—damnyankees at other times," Great-uncle Rudd said. "Them Yankees charged the men beside the church and found they was too strong for 'em, so they halted."

"Where were you and Mr. Puttiphut?" asked Graham. "Were you at the church or in the cornfield or in the pasture?"

The old man laughed. "Me and Clee wasn't any of them places. But we was nearby, Tuck. Us Texans heard the firin' of guns and cannons but didn't pay no great heed to it. We'd fought battles before. We reckoned there'd be so many battles before the South won the war that we'd be weary of 'em. Right now at Sharpsburg, we figgered the other Confederate soldiers would deal with the damnyankees this time without callin' on us for our help. Other Southerners besides Texans could fight right smartly too, when they set their minds to it. We were willin' to grant 'em that."

Great-uncle Hoyt smiled at his brother and said, "Rudd, you jest used that word you said nobody was ever to say here."

"What word, Hoyt?"

"Grant."

"I take it back then. Quit interruptin' my story, all of you. Let me tell you about us Texas men. We was fixin' to have breakfast, and it promised to be one to remember. We'd been issued some fryin' meat, the first fryin' meat we'd had all week long. I surely had my taster set for that meat. It turned out to be a breakfast I never ate but remembered all the same. We Texans was called up in a hurry and told to bring our rifles. We went into battle without gettin' that meat into us at all. You see, a Yankee general had put three cannons on a ridge lookin' out over that cornfield full of Confederate soldiers." The old man shook his head sadly. "What them blue-belly cannon done to them poor devils in that cornfield ain't nothin' to talk about to innocent young uns like the pair of you, let me tell you. Them Yankee cannons slew them fine Southern lads in the corn by the hunderds, mowin' them down with cannonballs, with the cornstalks fallin' around 'em too. Then the Yankees came rollin' on to the church.

"And there waitin' for the blue bellies now was me and Clee and Hood's brigade of Texas men. We was ragin' mad. Of course, that was because we hadn't had the time to eat the fryin' meat for breakfast. It's dangerous to come between a Texan and his food. Me and Clee and them other Texans was in the mood for fightin'. Bullets buzzed like bees in the scrub there, and we fought like fiends. We took them advancin' Yankees apart. Yellin' our heads off with 'Ee-yah-ee-yah' till our throats was raw, we chased them blue bellies away. Their general even took a bullet in his foot. It was Clee who done that, shootin' low to put that general out of action and not kill him.

"And then their cannon started hittin' us. That was

bad, hellish bad, for us. Sharpsburg was a cannon hell, let me tell you. Long as I live, and it is long gone by now, I'll never forget them great big guns thunderin' up on that ridge, firin' and firin' until the iron barrels of 'em was red-hot. Brave Confederate boys got cut down that day by the thousands! You see, we wasn't only fightin' without breakfast. We was gettin' a mite weary. The Yankees that kept a-comin' was fresh as mornin' dew. I can close my eyes and still see 'em comin' with their rifles and bayonets. They advanced on us howlin', 'Hurrah, boys, hurrah,' which was their battle cry."

Just as if he was listening, Great-uncle Rudd closed his eyes, but he opened them quickly when Graham asked, "You lost the battle?"

"Tuck, nobody knows for sure who lost or who won there. Soldiers are still arguin' about Sharpsburg, I reckon. It was a sort of draw. When the Yankees finally fell back, half of us Texas men was killed or wounded. I got a little bit winged by a blue-belly bullet, myself, so I fell back with the Texans to rest up for a spell. Old Clee wasn't even scratched."

"Did that Yankee bullet hit you in the ear?" Graham wanted to know.

"No, it nicked me in the calf of the leg, ruinin' one of my boots. Well, this battle went on and on. More Yankees came in fresh all the time, whole divisions of 'em, and we beat 'em back, though we was quite weary by now." Great-uncle Rudd touched the top of his left ear, shook his head again, and said, "I got to hand it to 'em. Them Yankees put up a good scrap there—almos' as good as ours. All day long we Confederates fought, and all day long the blue bellies fought too. By nightfall the battlefield was full of wounded, dyin', and already dead Confederates and Yankees. We'd fought like hell for twelve hours in the bloodiest battle the Civil War was ever to have, though we didn't know it at the time.

"Me and Clee sat under some trees in the dark listenin' to the pitiful callin' and cryin' of the wounded men out there. They was cryin' 'Help me' and 'Water,' but nobody dared to go out to help 'em 'cause everybody figgered the battle wasn't over yet. Anybody who crawled out there coulda been shot dead too. Besides I had only one boot because, as I said, the bullet that had nicked my leg had shot one whole side of the boot away. Let me tell you, losin' that there boot was a big worry to me, and it led to lots of trouble.

"I recall Clee sayin' to me, 'You got to get yourself another pair of boots, Rudd, fast as you can. You can't go around Maryland like that.'

"I told him, 'I know it, Clee. I talked to the supply officer about it. He ain't got any boots my size with high heels. I got a small and delicate-shaped foot. There ain't nothin' worse than boots that don't fit good. The wrong boots can make a man's life a misery.'

" 'That's so, Rudd,' old Clee said to me. 'You'll jest have to stomp along best as you can on one boot.' Then he asked me, 'What do you think General Lee's goin' to do tomorrow?'

"I said, 'I dunno, Clee. Fight some more, I reckon.'

"But General Lee didn't do that. Pretty soon we all went back over the Potomac River, but let me tell you, I can never forget Sharpsburg and them cannons. I went away with General Lee and General Hood and Clee Puttiphut knowin' in my heart that I'd fought well and stood well at Sharpsburg, though I was limpin' because of my nicked leg and missin' boot. I was truly footsore then."

"But you haven't told us yet about your ear!" my brother complained.

"Say, Tuck, I haven't, have I? And that sad event took place at Sharpsburg, didn't it?"

"I think that's what you said, Great-uncle Rudd," I answered.

"Yep, Missy, I got to recollect on this a bit further." After saying that, the old man was quiet for a time while we listened to the soft murmuring of Grandmother's and Mrs. Hemmrich's voices out in the kitchen. Then Rudd Quiney began again. "I lost my ear after the battle like I told you. I lost it because of them boots I needed."

"Boots? You got your new boots then?" I asked.

"Well, no, not right then. This is how it was. There was a little Yankee major layin' on the ground in the woods Clee and me was comin' through after Sharpsburg. We figured that he'd crawled there by himself, or somebody had fetched him there to die of his wounds. The Yankee appeared to both me and Clee to be dead. And because of his bein' dead, he didn't have no need for them new shinin' boots he was wearin'. I surely had a need for 'em, though. So me and Clee come up to him and stood over him. There was a shiny sword layin' beside his hand too. Clee had his eye on that for a souvenir, but I had no use for it. All I could see was them boots. Glory be, they appeared to be my size, even if they was a mite low in the heels.

"So, I bent down over the major and commenced tuggin' at one of them fine boots. But then to my surprise, up flew that little Yankee's eyelids. 'Who the devil are you, and what do you think you're up to?' he barked at me.

"Being Texas-courteous, I said to him, still bending over him with one hand on the heel of his left boot, 'I do beg your pardon, sir. I'd thought you'd gone above.'

"Clee, standin' behind me, explained what I'd said to that Yankee officer. 'My pardner here means to say that he believed you had gone to heaven.'

" 'Well, I haven't! I'm not ready to go just yet.' And as I was straightening up, that major grabbed his sword and swung it up. Neat as could be, he sliced off part of my left ear. I hastened off as fast as I could before he could cut away all the ear or some other parts of me. Clee didn't waste time neither. We left that blue-belly major with his sword and with his boots. We coulda shot him, but it wouldn't have been the kind of thing a Texan from Santa Rosa County would do. That woulda been stealin'."

"What happened after that?" I asked.

"I made it back to Hood's Brigade with a part of me

gone forever. And I got some boots elsewhere the next day. I don't recall anymore where or how. Me and Clee stayed with General Hood and was with him at another battle where he lost the use of his arm. We was still with him at another battle where he was wounded again and had his leg cut off. But in spite of them losses John B. Hood kept on fightin'."

"My goodness!" was all I could say.

Great-uncle Hoyt put in, "That part about General Hood's bein' wounded so often is gospel truth."

"It surely is." Great-uncle Rudd came in fast. "Old General Hood wasn't with Lee, though, on that sad and mournful day when Lee finally had to give up the war to the damnyankees, in 1865."

"Neither was you or Clee, Rudd," said Great-uncle Hoyt very softly, with his hands resting on his knees. He was rocking in his chair with an unlit cigar in his mouth.

"No, I wasn't. I got wounded in my right hind foot by a minié ball in the same battle where Hood lost his leg. So I had to quit fightin'. But I heard all about the end of the war from men who was still fightin' in 1865."

Graham asked, "What happened to your friend, Clee Puttiphut?"

"He rode back to Texas too. The lucky cuss came through the whole war with nothin' worse than a chigger bite. And that was the end of warrin' and scrappin' for the two of us sons of Texas. We never took part in any more wars, though we had some other very interestin' dealings together."

Then I heard Grandmother's voice as she approached. "Merle, Graham, your mother wants me to show you where the bathroom is so you can wash up from the trip. It's out on the back porch here." I saw how her eyes went suspiciously from Hoyt to Rudd and back again as she stood in the doorway.

"Tell me, Sue," Rudd asked her, "was you ever sorry that you didn't get married up with old Clee Puttiphut?"

"Good Lord, no! That runty, little, two-legged coyote? He never even seriously tried to court me. He was two years younger than you were, Rudd, and that would have made him born in 1858, and I was born in 1855. Why, Clee Puttiphut was a whole three years younger than I was. I never even looked at him. It seemed to me that he'd never been anywhere and would never go anywhere, either."

Graham exclaimed, "Oh, he went lots and lots of places! He and Great-uncle Rudd were together back East during the Civil War."

Grandmother put a hand on each side of the door. Then she started to laugh. "Graham Tucker, can't you add and subtract at all? The Civil War was fought during the years 1861 and 1865. Your Great-uncle Rudd was all of five years old when it began and nine years old when it ended." She paused and turned to Rudd. "Rudd, are you *still* telling that story of how you lost part of your ear?"

My brother and I stared at Rudd Quiney. He was grinning and not looking one bit sheepish or embarrassed the way he should have.

"Sue, it's still a danged good story. Your young uns swallowed it hook, line, and sinker."

"You haven't changed your spots one bit, Rudd. Hoyt, has he improved at all?"

"Not much, Susie," agreed Hoyt.

She sighed. Her words were for Graham and me. "Don't you take anything you hear from my little brother as gospel, you hear? Take everything he says with a grain of salt." She crooked her finger at us. "Come along now, you two."

As I followed her down a dark, little stairway that smelled of mothballs, I asked her, softly so nobody else would hear me except Graham, "Does your brother Rudd tell lies all of the time?"

"Merle, that's a question every Quiney relation of his in Texas has been asked at least twice. As far as I know, not one of us has had a surefire answer. All we know for certain is that we are in agreement that Rudd is the black sheep of the family. He has humiliated just about every one of us one way or another over the years."

"What did he do to you, Grandmother?"

"That's a secret between him and me."

"Is it the reason why you haven't seen him since 1881?"

"Indeed it is, and don't you dare ask me any more about it, you hear?"

I changed the subject. "What does Mrs. Hemmrich say about Mom's wrist?"

"It has to be soaked a lot. Well, Floy's had her first

adventure already on this trip, hasn't she? I keep telling her to look on her injury that way, and you two keep thinking the same thing. It's an adventure. It will make the time here pass for you more quickly."

Graham had caught up with us. He was smiling when he asked, "Grandma, will we really be here in MacRae for five days?"

"I'm afraid that's so. Why, Graham, you sound as if you actually like it here!"

"Well, I like being called Tuck. I always hated being called Graham, you know, even if it was Dad's mother's maiden name. And I liked hearing Rudd talk about the Civil War. Some of what he said wasn't lies. I know because I read about some of those things in school. What's more, Great-uncle Hoyt said out on the veranda that he and Great-uncle Rudd couldn't read at all, so what Rudd says has to be true, doesn't it? How else would he know all that?"

"They can't read or write, but Rudd's heard a lot about the war from the time he was your age. He's often listened to men who were real soldiers talking. However, his knowing something about the Civil War doesn't make his whoppers any easier to take in my opinion."

"But how did he really lose part of his ear?" I asked. "Do you know?"

"No, I don't know for sure, Merle. All that I know for a fact is that when I saw him in 1881 it was missing at the time."

I said, "My, but that was a long, long time ago."

"So it was, Merle."

5

My Brother Went A-Courtin'

While we washed our hands and then our faces, with Grandmother checking to see that we did it right, I asked her, "Has anybody ever called Great-uncle Rudd a liar to his face?"

"Lots of people have when they heard that story of the Yankee officer and the sword, but it doesn't do any good. It doesn't faze him one bit to be called a liar or a fibber or a storyteller. He just grins to hear the names people call him. Some of them get mad, but it's no use. Far as I know, he's never gotten into a fight over his stories."

As Graham dried his hands, he said, "Honestly, Grandma, doesn't *anyone* know the true story about the ear?"

"Not anyone that I know about—unless perhaps Hoyt does."

"I think Great-uncle Rudd likes me," my brother went on. "Could I ask him again—for the real story this time?"

"You can ask and see what happens, Graham."

"Call me Tuck, please. That's going to be my name from now on. A real, true cowboy gave it to me." All at once, with the towel still in one hand, he asked, "Was he a real, true cowboy once upon a time?" He sounded plenty worried.

"Yes, he was. I can vouch for that. Didn't I tell you that already?"

"That's good." Graham put the towel back on the rack again. "If anybody back home in California ever calls me anything but Tuck from now on, I'm going to punch him in the nose."

"Gracious, Graham, I mean Tuck," said Grandmother laughing. "It didn't take my brothers long to bring the Quiney out in you, did it? They're like a disease. They generally make me feel yeasty, too, so I can't criticize you. How about you, Merle? How did Rudd and Hoyt affect you?"

"I don't know for sure yet," I told her. "I think I like Great-uncle Hoyt, but I have my doubts about Great-uncle Rudd. He seems to favor boys over girls. I think he likes Tuck better than me."

She nodded. "Yes, that makes sense. As far as I know, the only woman he ever did get along really well with was Ruby Nell. Mrs. Hemmrich knew her, too, better than I did. I only met her once or twice."

"Who's Ruby Nell?" I wanted to know.

"Ruby Nell Puttiphut. She was Rudd's wife. She died back in 1899 or thereabouts. He wasn't married to her for more than a couple of years. After she died, he moved in here with Hoyt, and they hired Mrs. Hemmrich to come up from Santa Rosa County to keep house for them."

I felt my head was spinning with all the dates I'd heard that day. I'd heard about the 1850's and Civil War days and the 1880's and now the 1890's. No wonder old people seemed absentminded sometimes. They had so much to remember and so many dates to keep straight. And, of course, Great-uncle Rudd had confused me, too, talking about the Civil War he'd never been in.

Well, at least I knew for sure that now it was 1929.

Dinner was chicken-fried steak and fried onions and fried potatoes that our great-uncles really tore into. But there was a big bowl of collard greens, too, and a very good lemon pie. I'd never eaten a better pie. The two Quiney men didn't touch the greens at all, though each of them had two slices of the pie.

"They've got a sweet tooth, both of them," I heard Mrs. Hemmrich tell Mom, who sat beside me with her wrist bandaged so tight it was puffing above it and below it. Mom didn't say much to anyone at dinner, and right afterwards she told us that she felt ill and if nobody minded she'd go right up to bed. Nobody said they minded, so off Mom went without even saying goodnight to anyone.

As we folded our napkins to put into the rings Mrs. Hemmrich had set aside at each place, Grandmother said to Graham and me, "Children, we have to make do here because there's only one guest room. Your mother and I will take that. You two will sleep in the Studebaker . . . and Brownie, too. There'll be bedding out there for you."

Sleep in the car? That was exciting! Tuck said, "You take the back seat, Merle, and you take Brownie. I'll take the front."

I nodded. I supposed I'd have to fuss over the dog quite a bit before she'd go to sleep. She was used to sleeping in Grandmother's room—and a lot of time on the foot of her bed. Brownie didn't seem to be as welcome here as we were, and I wasn't at all sure that I liked that. All the time Great-uncle Rudd had been telling us about his fake Civil War experiences Brownie had been out in the kitchen, and now during dinner she was shut up out on a screened porch full of plants in pots.

So I asked Great-uncle Hoyt, not Great-uncle Rudd, "Don't you like dogs?"

He smiled at me. "It ain't me that has feelin's about dogs. It's Rudd here."

"Why don't you like dogs, Great-uncle Rudd?"

"Because I never seen a dog that could come up to one I had when I was a young snort. His name was Slacker. He was as big as a small horse and could keep up with a gallopin' racer any day of the week."

"Rudd," said Mrs. Hemmrich, "no one will believe that."

"For short distances old Slacker truly could, but I

don't intend to talk about him right now or talk about dogs the size of earwigs that yap too much." He jerked his thumb toward the back porch where poor Brownie was yipping now out of loneliness. "But your askin' me about dogs, Missy, put me in mind of a trip I took a long time back with Clee Puttiphut, who'd jest lost his dog from snakebite and needed some jollyin' up. So when my big brother Earl took it into his head to go to Fort Worth and asked me to go along with him, I asked Clee to come too. Me and Clee hoped to have some fun in Fort Worth, but it didn't turn out that way. Thanks to Earl's courtin' a gal, I come to lose part of my left ear."

"Is this true or is it another story?" Graham asked suspiciously.

"It's gospel truth, Tuck. If Carolina'll fetch in my arthuritis medicine, I'll pour myself a big glass of it and tell you about what happened back in 1876 in Fort Worth."

Mrs. Hemmrich sighed. Then she and Grandmother got up, one after the other, but before she left the room, Grandmother said, "Yes, 1876. That year would make you twenty years old, Rudd. I'd left home, myself, the year before so you know that I can't contradict this story, can I?" She was giving him a hard look.

"No, you wouldn't be knowin' about me and Clee in Fort Worth." He was grinning again as he called after her.

In a minute or so both ladies were back again. There was a yellow-colored glass in Mrs. Hemmrich's hand.

"What was in the jug you poured that from, Carolina?" asked Grandmother. "You made such a face when you uncorked it."

Her old friend sighed again. "Alfalfa tea, honey, vinegar, and whiskey—but mostly whiskey."

"Rudd Quiney!" Grandmother's voice was very sharp. She was really angry. "Lord in heaven, Rudd, you know that there's prohibition in this country these days! It's against the law to drink alcohol or even to have it in the house. The sheriff of this county could come to this house and put us all in jail."

"It ain't alcohol, Sue. It's jest my special medicine to put some oil in my joints."

"Carolina," asked Grandmother, "where does he get the whiskey? If we can't stop him from drinking it, maybe we can find out where he gets it. Then we can report the bootlegger who sells it to him to the sheriff and put that man in prison."

"Oh, Susannah, Rudd makes it himself. I don't know where his moonshine still is hidden. I make the tea, honey, and vinegar mix for him, and he pours in the whiskey. That way I don't take any part in breaking the law."

"Good Lord, I hope not! It's fate again. There must be a lesson in life for me to make me come here. I'll have to decide what it is."

"Oh, Grandma," came from Tuck, "why are you going on so? You know Dad makes home-brew beer back home in Pasadena. You helped him put the yeast in it yourself."

"E-yah-ya-yaw-yaw!" A loud screeching sound came from Great-uncle Rudd, who took off his hat and waved it in the air the way somebody would who was cheering. Then he cried out, "You tell 'em, Tuck, boy!"

When Grandmother opened her mouth to say something, the old man let out the same yell to drown out her words. Finally she threw her hands up in the air and left with Mrs. Hemmrich a couple of steps behind her. My, but the housekeeper gave Rudd a furious glance!

When they were gone, he told us, "That there was the famous old Rebel yell. You don't hear that much anymore, I guess."

"I never heard it," said my brother. "It's true that Grandmother put the yeast in the beer, but Dad told her it was root beer. He fooled her."

Great-uncle Hoyt had to be the slowest eater I ever saw and his brother one of the fastest. Hoyt was still on his second piece of pie. He said, "It's good to know that Susannah doesn't make beer."

Rudd took a deep swallow of the glass of "medicine," wiped his mouth with the back of his hand, and said, "Ah. Where was I now? Them women sure give me a hard time. It's a sad thing when a man ain't master in his own house, ain't it, Hoyt?"

"It's my house, Rudd, remember? I won it in that Dallas poker game and hung on to it ever afterwards. Now, Rudd, you was tellin' these here two about you and Clee and our brother Earl when Earl was gallin'—courtin' gals—around in Fort Worth."

"So I was. But me and Clee weren't gallin'. I never looked at any calico at all after I once set eyes on Ruby Nell, and because Clee was with me and Ruby Nell was his sister, I didn't dare gal around one bit in Fort Worth."

Great-uncle Hoyt nodded and put down his fork. "That's how it was with me, too, as you may recall. Once a little old black-haired gal cornered me at a square dance and asked me to pull in double harness with her for the rest of our days. Because I was forced to tell her 'No,' I never messed with calico again neither." I watched him peer down into his coffee cup, pour in some cream, drop in three lumps of sugar, and then lower his right thumb down into the cup and begin to stir. "Git on with how you lost part of your ear, Rudd. We're all a-listenin'."

"How about you, Missy?" asked Great-uncle Rudd.

"Yes, sir," I said, tearing my eyes from Hoyt's thumb. "We're all ears, all of us. Can't you tell?" And then I was horrified at what I'd said.

He only laughed. Leaning back so far in his chair that I was sure it was going to tip over, he said very, very softly, "Billy bedamned, long gone by it was, but I recall them days in Fort Worth like they were yesterday. Well, Earl, he had took it into his head that he needed a wife. It wasn't that he wanted somebody to cuddle up to and say sweet nothin's to day and night. There was more to it than sweet stuff. The fact was that he had his hands full runnin' a mule-and-horse ranch and didn't have the time to ride herd on the rest of us

Quineys. There musta been nine or ten of us still to home at the time, rangin' from Earl's growed-up age to Lucy's bein' not much more than a weaner yet. You see, our ma had died jest a little bit after Lucy, the last of the Quineys, got borned. So in the worst way Earl needed a gal to look after the tribe of Quineys."

Rudd took another sip of his medicine and went on. "Earl had looked over the crop of gals the right age in Santa Rosa County, but not one of them was willin' to marry him, because they knowed too much about the herd of us at home. So we, Earl, me, and Clee Puttiphut, rode to Fort Worth where nobody knowed us personally."

"We Quincys was somethin' of a handful them days," said Great-uncle Hoyt. "As I recall, it was because there was so many of us that your Grandma Sue left home to work for that there schoolmarm in the town of Cottonwood. It was that schoolmarm who taught Sue to read and write. That's how come she knows how to and Rudd and me don't, though the younger uns in the family had to go to school in spite of their opposition to it."

While I sat wondering about Grandmother's unusual schooling—this was something she'd never told us about—I thought I understood now why she was always talking about how important a good education was. That was because she'd had to pick hers up along the way. I wondered if Mom knew about this.

Then Great-uncle Rudd said, "I'm glad you reminded

me of readin' and writin'. That was the other reason Earl went courtin' to find a gal. He needed one who could write and read and figger out arithmetic enough to help him in the horse-and-mule business. Most Santa Rosa County gals couldn't do that no more than he could, though Ruby Nell could somewhat.

"I couldn't see that Earl needed a meddlin' female around our ranch, so I went along with him and Clee to town in hopes of dashin' Earl's hopes of marryin'."

"Yes, sir, a Fort Worth woman mighta made us Quineys mind our manners," said Hoyt, after putting his thumb into his coffee cup again as a stirrer.

Rudd went on. "We drove twenty-five big, mean-natured mules all the way north to town and left 'em there in a corral for sale. The Army wanted Texas mules bad, and they was offerin' a good price for the lot right then and there. But would Earl take their offer? Not him. He wanted time to do some courtin'. I couldn't talk him into gettin' the mule money and leavin'. He'd figgered that he could get the same price the next week. He was givin' hisself one whole week to catch a bride in. That was all the time he could spare, because if he stayed away any longer, he might find when he got home that some of the Quineys there had scalped and murdered the other ones. He'd left Varne in charge, and Varne was only a scrub of a kid then."

Tuck interrupted, "We've met Great-uncle Varne. Why didn't Earl leave you at home if you were older? Or why didn't he leave Great-uncle Hoyt?"

Hoyt answered, "I wasn't at home then, Tuck. I was elsewhere. And Rudd had to go to stop Earl from matrimony. It was Rudd's duty."

"As I saw it, it surely was, Hoyt. Earl got us all a room at the Saint Charles Hotel, and then he headed direct for a tonsorial parlor to get a bath and a shave and his hair cut. After that, he went to a merchandise emporium and bought hisself new boots and a new Stetson hat and a new shirt and vest and pants. When he came back, me and Clee scarce knowed him for my brother—he looked so different and smelled so good. I grabbed ahold of him and sniffed him till he said, 'Leggo of me, you worthless galoot.' Then he give me and Clee our orders. He could do that because he was not only older than we was, he was a lot bigger too. We was to keep out of saloons and behave ourselves and not rile him while he was settlin' down to serious courtin'. Earl was inclined to take things very serious a lot of the time.

"Earl had decided that the best huntin' ground for a bride would be in the churches. So even if it was Thursday night and that rip-roarin' city of sin was goin' full toot havin' itself a good time, me and Clee had to go with Earl to a prayer meetin'. It was at six o'clock at a Baptist Church. The three of us got there early, took off our hats out of respect, and took a back seat so Earl could get a good view of the congregation. Them Baptists disappointed him. There wasn't any gals there that was the right age and had the good looks that suited him except for one that had too much white in her eye for comfort. That scared Earl off."

I watched Great-uncle Hoyt nod as he stirred. "That's how a man judges the nature of a horse—by how much white shows when the horse rolls its eyes. It's the mark of a mean brute or of a scared one, and no gal like that would be a fittin' wife for a Quiney. Rudd was right about that."

"Really and truly, is that so about horses?" asked my brother.

"Really and truly, Tuck," Rudd Quiney told him. "The Methodists had their prayer meetin' at seven thirty, so we took that in too that night, at their church down the street. Their seats weren't no softer than the Baptists' was, and because the Baptists had already started up saddle sores on us, we fidgeted even more with the Methodists. There was four gals there that Earl claimed might do, though I naturally didn't agree. I whispered to him durin' a hymn that one gal was a mite walleyed, another one was almost a midget in size, and the third one was uglier than a mud fence plastered over with frogs. Try as I might, though, I couldn't find no fault with the looks of the fourth one, Miss Avarilla Arrowwood. She had long yaller curls and big brown eyes and a noticeable nose, and she had duded herself up in pink calico to show off all her handsomeness. It appeared to me and Clee that she was doin' exactly what Earl was doin'—huntin'. The way that gal looked over the men's half of the congregation was somethin' to see. When

Earl showed all the teeth in his head in a big hello smile at her during the next hymn, she smiled back at him and nodded like she already knowed him. Me and Clee, we give her some sour stares, but she didn't pay us no mind. It was him she was after. And when he looked at her, he grinned like a mule eating a prickly pear.

"As we left the prayer meetin', she passed us by goin' out the door, walkin' behind her ma and pa. The two of them old people nodded friendly like to us strangers, but that little gal smiled like sunrise again. She sure smelled to heaven of some flower odor. You shoulda seen Earl sniffin' it. It was more powerful than all the barber's bay rum on him. Otherwise, he could never havc smelled it.

"After she'd gone off with her folks, Earl shook hands with the preacher outside the church and asked, 'Who's the holy-looking gent with the stovepipe hat?' Meanin' the girl's pa. Earl was clever at times.

" 'That's Mr. Arrowwood. That was his wife with him and his daughter, Avarilla. Will we be seeing you, sir, in church come Sunday morning? You and them fine young men with you are surely very welcome here.'

" 'You bet we'll be here,' Earl promised him. And our hearts sank.

"Down in the street I asked, 'Where are you gonna look for a wife the rest of the night, Earl?'

" 'Nowhere, Rudd. I've found the one I set my heart on. She's Miss Avarilla Arrowwood.'

"I told him then, 'You make up your mind danged fast, Earl.'

"'As I see it, Rudd, I got to. If I can get hitched to Avarilla Arrowwood by Tuesday, I can maybe be home with her before all hell breaks loose down on the ranch.'

"I went on. 'By Tuesday, Earl? But you ain't ever spoken with her yet.'

"Billy bedamned, I jest couldn't stop Earl nohow. He said he was goin' to get a box of fudge and a bunch of posies to her by Friday noon, if he could buy them fancy things in Fort Worth.

"Next mornin' bright and early he sent off me and Clee to hunt 'em up while he went on down to the mule market and from there to a store to look for a weddin' ring. We was able, me and Clee, to talk him out of doing any ring buyin' as bein' the sort of bold thing that would scare a gal out of a year's growth if a man sprung a ring on her that fast.

"Me and Clee had some trouble with them posies and fudge, as I recall. We couldn't find no place at all to buy anythin' but horehound and licorice and peppermint candy, and the only posies anywhere in Fort Worth was so far behind somebody's front fence we didn't dare reach through the pickets and jerk 'em loose, because we was ordered by Earl to behave ourselves. Earl, he was awful big. So finally me and Clee put our heads together and decided on somethin' that'd do jest as good as fudge and flowers. We got a bottle of whiskey and a box of cheroots with Earl's cash and hired a boy who knowed Fort Worth real good to take 'em to the Arrowwood house as comin' from Mr. Earl Beauregard Quiney of Santa Rosa County."

DIXON PUBLIC LIBRARY
DIXON, ILLINOIS

I couldn't help asking, "What are cheroots?" I thought to myself that whiskey was a terrible present to send a girl, but didn't say so.

"Cigars, Missy. We figgered that if we couldn't give pleasure to the gal we could give joy to her pa. They was good cheroots, and the whiskey was good enough to cut the alkali in the drinkin' water for the whole Arrowwood family for a week at least. Pleasin' her pa would give Earl the inside track with Avarilla too, as much as plyin' her sweet tooth and charmin' her nose. We didn't tell Earl what we sent. He moped around the Saint Charles Hotel the rest of Friday and all day long Saturday, mostly settin' out on the veranda hopin' to get a glimpse of Avarilla walkin' past and jest waitin' for Sunday to roll around. He was almost beside hisself with nervous fits in church that day. He sat there durin' the sermon with his eyes fixed on her across the way. He was surely in high hopes of bein' asked to supper at the Arrowwood house.

"And so he was. Her pa came up to him jest after the services and said in our hearin', 'Mr. Quiney, I want to thank you for what you sent over to me. You're a man of good taste, the sort of man I like to do business with. I take it somebody in your family come up here to town to see a doctor.' Mr. Arrowwood was lookin' around big Earl, starin' at me and Clee like we was sick unto death.

" 'Well, sir,' Earl said next, lookin' puzzled, 'nobody's sick at all. I jest wanted to make your family's acquaintance, that's all.'

"Mr. Arrowwood answered, 'You've done that, my boy. My wife and little gal and I would be honored if you'd take supper with us this afternoon. I take it you aim to quit the mule-and-horse business? Naturally, I made inquiries about you here in town. The name of Quiney is not unknown in these parts. Do you plan to settle down here and go into business—maybe my business—once you've sold them mules of yours and made a handsome profit?'

" 'No, sir. What is your business anyhow?'

" 'Undertakin'. I trust I don't sound too proud in sayin' that I bury jest about everyone of any importance who dies here in Fort Worth.'

"Now this took old Earl back a bit, lemme tell you. It knocked him right back on his hocks, as a matter of fact. Then he caught sight of Avarilla smilin', standin' with her ma under a white ruffledy parasol, and he said, 'I'd be plumb proud to come to supper at your house.'

" 'Fine, Mr. Quiney, you be there at three o'clock then, and we'll show you how good our little Avarilla cooks up a chicken. You can't miss the place. There's a big sign out front that has my name on it in black letters.'

" 'I'll be there,' said Earl, who was standin' with his hat over his chest lookin' after the gal, who was walkin' away lookin' back over her shoulder at him from under that parasol. She was surely givin' him a come-hither glance.

"He went hither too," continued Great-uncle Rudd after another swig of his arthritis medicine. "He left me and Clee at the hotel, and, duded up fit to kill and stinkin' to high heaven of bay rum, he sashayed out to court Avarilla. He'd told me and Clee to mind what we did in town and not get in any fusses with anybody, or he'd take it unkindly. He reckoned he would have good news for us when he got back to the hotel.

"Yes, siree, everything was workin' out jest fine for him and jest rotten for me. Him and Avarilla took to each other like climbin' vines to the side of a shingled house. He was goin' to rent a buggy the next day and take her ridin' out over the prairie in the mornin', and that night he was squirin' her to a square dance. About this time I asked him what he planned to do about showin' me and Clee a good time in Fort Worth. We hadn't once cut our wolf loose in town. We'd perched on the porch of our hotel like we was in Sunday school. All Earl would say was that it was our own danged fault. He said that we knew from the start he'd come to town to pursue a purpose, and there wasn't no reason to cuss him out now because he was pursuin' it purposefully. And that night when he was going to bed he took his hat off first when he undressed. That proved to us that all this courtin' had fevered his brain. Cowboys never do that. Cowboys take their hat off last of all and put it on first thing in the mornin'. We had to do somethin' fast, Clee and me, to keep Earl out of the arms of a gal he hardly knowed. We had to rescue Earl from hisself. We decided that we had to take a hand in his courtin'."

"That's terrible," I couldn't help saying.

Great-uncle Rudd either didn't understand me or pretended that he didn't. He said, "You bet it was, Missy. We had to do somethin' quick as ever we could to get Earl out of that mess."

"What did you and Clee do?" asked my brother. By gosh, his eyes were round with believing. I wanted to kick him, but he was too far away from my foot, across the table.

"Me and Clee put our heads together and got a good idea goin'. While Earl courted Avarilla Arrowwood out in the buggy on the prairie, Clee went to visit the preacher of the Methodist Church and tell him that Earl had come close to bein' hanged for horse theft last year and had been let go by the judge only out of pity because Earl was the head of a big family of poor orphans. Clee told the preacher that the Arrowwoods ought to be told this. While Clee was doin' that, I called on Mrs. Arrowwood and told her some facts. I said that Earl wanted a gal to keep house for him more than he wanted a wife and that there were nine Quineys at home at the last count and they were a mighty ornery lot. I figgered that should end the sudden romance right then and there."

"What did the minister and Mrs. Arrowwood say?" I asked. This story was getting worse and worse. And now I believed every awful word of it, because I was sure it was just what Rudd would have done.

"Not what me and Clee expected." Great-uncle Rudd was scowling. "The preacher told Clee that many a man had repented when he got a good sight of the rope that was goin' to hang him. And Avarilla's ma said to me that her daughter was a real strong gal, who jest doted on ornery kids and who craved a tribe of her own kids."

Graham laughed while I kept a straight face. I was getting more and more annoyed.

The old man went on. "Me and Clee did some deep thinkin', and because I'd seen the Arrowwood house and undertakin' parlor I decided what we was going to do. We were goin' to wait in the dark till Earl and the gal come back from the square dance, and we'd listen in on 'em alongside the veranda while Earl popped the question to her about marryin' up with him. There was a sofa out there right close to a honeysuckle-covered ladder contraption."

Graham explained, "A trellis is what it's called. Mom hit one once with her car."

"Well, me and Clee was posted jest at the side of the ladder, out of sight, when up came them two laughin' and singin' and holdin' hands. Sure as could be, they sat down on that sofa. You could hear it near bust under Earl's weight, and that Fort Worth gal wasn't such a little mite of a thing neither. For a time they was quiet as mice, doin' nothin' but lettin' out sighs. Then came a sound that surprised me and Clee, the clickin' of knittin' needles. And then I recalled a wicker basket set down near the sofa. It musta had Avarilla's knittin' for winter inside it.

"All at once I heard Earl say, 'You know, you're purtier than a thirty-dollar pony wearin' a eighteen-dollar silver bridle.'

"It appeared to me that Avarilla had a voice like a gate hinge. She said over the clickin' noises, 'Oh, dear, Mr. Earl Quiney, you got to be the most charmin' man in all of Texas.'

"Well, if me and Clee had been dogs, that woulda give us runnin' fits—or worse. What they said afterwards was all mush and more mush. It didn't take long for Earl to get to the point, but he didn't exactly do it like he took a lot of pleasure in it. He sounded sort of strangled when he asked, 'How 'bout you marryin' up right away with me, Avarilla?'

" 'Oh, Earl!' The click-clicking sound stopped. 'I'm much too young for matrimony. What will my mother say to this?'

"Now I'd had a good look at Avarilla in broad daylight Sunday mornin' before she'd put up that there ruffledy parasol. She wasn't so young as she'd like folks to think she was. She was matrimony-minded all right. She couldn't afford to wait a lot longer, it seemed to me.

"She went on. 'I jest don't know what my mother will say when I tell her.'

"Well, I knew. I'd talked with her old ma. I figured her ma knew her better than Earl did, and her ma wasn't at all eager to hang on to her.

"So out of the middle of the honeysuckle, I said out loud, 'Good riddance is what she's goin' to say!'

"And then, holy snakes, it happened to me!

"I got stabbed right through the honeysuckle by Avarilla Arrowwood!"

"What with? Did Avarilla have a knife in her garter?"

Graham asked. There'd been a cowboy serial at the picture show not long ago where a dance-hall lady kept a toad-stabber dagger in one garter and a derringer pistol in the other.

"Nope. With one of them danged knittin' needles of hers. She stuck it straight out into the honeysuckle 'cause I'd surprised her so much—either that or because I'd made her so blamed mad. I never did learn which because of the ruckus that come afterwards. Naturally, I let out a howl that made her pull back the needle. That pullin' out hurt worse than goin' in. And after that Avarilla yelled and Clee yelled and Earl yelled and her ma and pa come boilin' out of the house. I could see through holes in the honeysuckle that her pa had a lamp in one hand and a shotgun in the other.

"Me and Clee didn't wait one instant. We lit out down the street and jumped over the Arrowwood fence into their backyard, where we hid ourselves beside a stack of wooden coffins until the hullabaloo was all over out front."

"What happened next?"

"Somethin' mighty mournful, Tuck. That stab in the dark with the knittin' needle made my ear infect. The bottom part pained me, swelled up, got red, then turned blue, and finally dark brown. One day, two weeks later, off it fell. I was plumb lucky I didn't die of lockjaw or poisoned blood."

"But what about your brother Earl?" I asked.

"That was the end of the courtin' he did that year in Fort Worth. Avarilla had a long talk with her ma, who told her about how many of us Quineys there was. Naturally, Earl hadn't told Avarilla that. Her ma also told Avarilla that she'd had a talk that mornin' with a colt of a redhead who had called hisself Rudd Quiney, and she was very sure now that there was quite a few crazy folks among the Quiney family. She was almost scared to have any daughter of hers living among them on a ranch so far from civilization.

"Earl had sort of lost heart in courtin'. The next day when Avarilla told him she agreed with her ma that she didn't want to get hitched jest yet—and so fast—he sold the mules. After that he took me and Clee around to the Centennial Theater to see a show and into two saloons, the Bon Ton and Friedburg's, where he bought us a glass of beer each. That's when he told us, sittin' in Friedburg's, that he'd decided Avarilla woulda been a mistake to marry up with after all. She'd been too quick on the draw with that knittin' needle. More than likely her nerves couldn't cope with nine of us Quineys. She'd keep flyin' off the handle at us.

"As all three of us rode happily out of Fort Worth together with the mule money in Earl's poke, I got the strong feelin' that he would never come straight out and say to me that he was pleased my hurt ear had saved him from marryin' in haste and bein' sorry for years afterwards. But he was pleased.

"Later on Earl did get married—to another gal from Fort Worth—but that was two years afterwards, and I wasn't around when he was courtin' her or things might have turned out different then too."

Great-uncle Rudd had finished his medicine down to the last drop, and he asked my brother, "Well, Tuck, how did you fancy this story of how I come to lose part of one ear?"

"I think I like it better than the Civil War one."

"Did you now?" Our great-uncle was grinning as he looked from Tuck's face to mine. I didn't smile back at him. The story held a person's attention all right. But there were parts of it I didn't like. And I couldn't put my finger exactly on what might be true and what not about it, but I felt sorry for Avarilla Arrowwood—and for Earl Quiney too.

6

Bear with Me Now...

That night as Brownie and I lay on the back seat of the Studebaker, I asked my brother, "Which one of Great-uncle Rudd's stories do you believe?"

"Neither one of them really. What about you, Merle?"

I patted Brownie, who was draped over my chest. "I don't know for sure, Graham. There are some things about both of them that could have happened. If he's lying, his face sure doesn't give him away. According to Grandmother and Mrs. Hemmrich, Great-uncle Rudd's so good at storytelling that people have asked him to enter prize contests for the Best Liars. But he won't do it."

"That's because he won't admit he isn't telling the truth. Besides he can't write. I think he'd feel too proud to ask anybody to write anything down on paper for him."

"Maybe it's more than that," I said. "If he writes them down for a lying contest, everybody will know they are lies. I think he wants people to believe him."

The rain had stopped, and the moon had come out, round as a California orange, to shine into the car and fill it with white light. It was hot. Grandmother had decided we wouldn't need more than a sheet and one thin blanket to be comfortable outside. She'd been right. The sun would probably be shining tomorrow, and it would be hot as blue blazes. Texas's summer climate wasn't much like Pasadena's. It seemed to me it got just as hot, but the heat here was wet and sticky.

"Merle," came my brother's voice again, "call me Tuck, huh?"

"I'll try to remember to, but I called you Graham for a long time before we came here." Brownie got down off me then to snuggle in the crook of my arm. "Mom's wrist and hand look really bad," I said. "I think Mrs. Hemmrich's right in saying she shouldn't try to drive for five days at least. That's going to mean we'll be here in MacRae for four more days. What are we going to do in all that time? There sure isn't much to MacRae."

He laughed and said, "We'll get to see Great-uncle Hoyt's horse, for one thing, and maybe ride it. And I've got a hunch that Great-uncle Rudd's got some more stories about where that missing part of his ear went to."

I nodded to the top of the Studebaker. "I'd bet on that. I wonder if we'll ever learn the true one."

"I don't know, but we can try to figure it out by figuring out which one can't be true. That story he told about Avarilla Arrowwood has to be a big fib, too, you know. I figured out what was wrong with it, didn't you?"

"No, but I tried to." I got up onto my elbow, disturbing Brownie and making her snuffle at me. "Do you know for sure? What did you figure out?"

"Merle, remember that Great-uncle Hoyt said that neither he nor Rudd nor Earl could read? Remember, too, that Rudd said Earl was supposed to find the Arrowwood's place in Fort Worth by reading the sign in black letters out in front of it? Well, Earl couldn't have found it that way if he couldn't read what was on a sign, could he?"

I sniffed. "Maybe Clee Puttiphut could read. Could he have shown Earl the way?"

"No. While you were helping Grandmother with the dishes out in the kitchen, I asked Great-uncle Hoyt if Clee Puttiphut could read and write. He said no, not only was Clee not a reader or a writer, Clee had never been known to be a thinker."

"Where does Clee live now?" I wanted to know.

"I asked Great-uncle Hoyt that, too, while Great-uncle Rudd was stuffing his jaw so full of tobacco he couldn't talk. Hoyt said that Clee had gone off to Alaska in 1898, when gold was first discovered there, and had never been heard of since. The rumor was that an avalanche had killed him."

"Well," I said, "then, nobody can check on his being in Great-uncle Rudd's tales if nobody knows where Clee Puttiphut is."

"That's right, Sis. Good night. Sleep tight, and don't let old Brownie's fleas bite."

I had the last word of the evening, though. "If one of them does, I'll grab the flea fast and throw it over the seat onto you, Tuck."

The next morning Brownie got me up by walking on me to the highest place, my hipbone. After that the dog put her front paws onto the back of the front seat, pushing down into me with her back feet and scrambled and crawled to the top of the seat. Up on top she gave out a "woof." Then down she went right on top of my brother.

Tuck let out a "woof" too and sat up all tousle-haired, but for once not grouchy. He'd changed in Texas. Clutching Brownie, he said, "Let's go ask about the horse they've got. Maybe Mom and Grandma aren't up yet, so we can see the horse before we have breakfast."

Neither of us much liked breakfast anyhow, so naturally I agreed. Then I remembered Brownie and shook my head. "I don't think we should take Brownie out to the barn, wherever it is. She's never set eyes on a horse. We'd better get her to Grandmother first."

"Oh, all right." Still in his pajamas and with his red bathrobe under one arm and Brownie under the other, Tuck headed for the house. It wasn't easy for me to slide into my green Chinese kimono with the peacocks on the back in the rear seat of the Studebaker, but I managed it. I got out of the car into the sunshine only a little while after he'd gone inside.

I had to pass both of my great-uncles, who were sitting in the parlor, waiting for breakfast, I supposed.

"My, my, ain't we all duded up in green this mornin' and purty as could be," said Great-uncle Hoyt.

Great-uncle Rudd had some more chewing tobacco in his cheek. He shifted it to the other side, spat into the cuspidor, and said, "Tuck's gone ahead of you to that newfangled bathroom Carolina made us build on to this house. By the way, he says that you don't fancy being called Missy much."

Darn Graham! He'd talked out of turn. I said, "My name's Merle."

"That ain't a real gal's name like Fanny or Ruth or Claramae," said Rudd Quiney. "What's your middle handle? I presume you got two of 'em."

"Yes, it's awful. It's Ora. That's worse than Missy."

"Purely awful. Yes, it is. Merle Ora. Oralee now woulda been a dandy name. Oralee is a purty song. What does them two names you got come out in initials?"

"Just Mo."

Great-uncle Hoyt said, "I knowed a man by the name of Mo back in Oklahoma Territory. He'd been a Texan, but he was forced to leave the state very suddenly. Rudd, should we call her that?"

"How 'bout it, little gal? How do you like that?"

"*Mo*?" It wasn't an everyday name exactly. I thought about it, then nodded. "Sure, it suits me all right, I guess. Better than Missy does." Great-uncle Rudd wasn't so bad after all—maybe.

"Mo, get yourself dressed and fed, and Hoyt and me will take you out to see his mare."

"Can Tuck and I ride her?"

"Nope, not right now," explained Hoyt Quiney. "She's got a warble under her saddle. Besides she may be old, but she's still a chestnut. Them chestnut horses is like redheaded gals, fiery-natured and touchy as sin. Always runnin' away from you if they can get the chance. Or carryin' you away with 'em. That's why Rudd and me give her the name of Susie."

I gasped, "You named her after Grandmother?"

"We surely did." Great-uncle Rudd winked at me. "But while she's here we're gonna call the mare Cinnamon to keep the peace. You won't tell on us, will you?"

"No." Grandmother might not like that too well, particularly if she found out why they'd named the mare after her.

She was out in the kitchen with Mrs. Hemmrich, standing at the stove next to her friend. Mom was up, too, soaking her wrist in a basin of water so hot it was steaming. Mom gave me a weak smile and asked how I'd taken to bedding down in the car. Then she told me she thought she'd spend most of the day lying down, taking aspirin tablets, and that she hoped Graham and I would behave ourselves. Brownie was at her feet eating from a bowl of food Mrs. Hemmrich had given her.

Grandmother turned around with a sausage stuck on a fork and asked, "Are you going to the barn with those brothers of mine to inspect old Susie this morning?"

She knew! Oh, this was terrible! I said fast to make her feel better. "They call her Cinnamon."

"The devil they do! They named her after me. Carolina told me." As she put the sausage down into the pan, she said, "Don't blush so, Merle, unless you're blushing for Rudd and Hoyt. I've seen the mare. She's a trim little thing. I figured my brothers would have a horse and that even if they are both too old and two spavined themselves to ride, they'd take good care of the animal. I'm not at all insulted by having a horse named after me. I like horses. Coming from them, it's more of a compliment. They've always been closer to horses than people."

Horses? Grandmother liked horses! She was surely full of surprises here in Texas. She had a sense of humor—a good one too!

Filled to the brim with nearly as many sausages and eggs as our great-uncles ate, my brother and I went off to the barn right after breakfast. It was a dim, dusky brown place that smelled nice. Susie was a little red-brown horse in a box stall. She knew our great-uncles, because she made a noise that Rudd said was a whinny of welcome. She let him rub her nose, but when we came near, she shied away from Tuck and me.

"She's got her little ways," said Hoyt, as he set a bucket of oats out of a bin down in front of her. "Jest you watch what she'll do now."

We Tuckers watched and saw the mare tip the bucket over with her nose so she could eat the grain off the boards. Next we saw her take some corn out of Hoyt's palm and noticed how she licked his palm all over with her long tongue afterwards.

Tuck asked, "Why did she lick your hand?"

"Because she's sayin' thank you for the corn and because of the salt on my hand. Horses jest love salt and sugar."

I asked my Great-uncle Rudd, "Why don't you have a horse too?"

"I did have one, Mo, but he got a twisted gut, and I had to put him out of his misery by shootin' him. Horses can get sick real easy. There's a lot to learn about horses. They can be the study of a lifetime, and still you don't know half of what's to be knowed about 'em. They're each and every one different—horses is."

We watched Susie eat the rest of the grain on the barn floor. Tuck asked, "Did you ever have a favorite horse? All of the cowboys we see at the picture shows have favorites."

"Surely, I did. A rawboned bay stallion by the name of Captain. There wasn't no better horse in all of California in the year of 1880."

"Were you out our way too?" asked my brother.

"Yes, siree, then and later on too. That's where I truly lost part of my ear—out in California. So you might say that a valuable part of Rudd Quiney was left in the state you folks live in."

"Gosh," exploded Tuck. "Out in California!" I couldn't tell if he was really impressed or just pretending to be, though I was watching him carefully.

Great-uncle Hoyt broke in, "I think I'd best get off my feet. Let's go over to the baled hay and sit down." He limped with his cane over to some bales set on the floor in a corner near some leather and metal straps hanging down from nails on the wall. They were pieces of buggy harness. There was a saddle placed on a sawhorse just under the straps on the wall, and some bridles hung among the leather pieces. I didn't know the names of the straps because I had never harnessed a horse.

"I wish we could ride Susie," I said. "I took riding lessons at a riding academy for a while back home, and I rode horses sometimes up in Bishop, California, on a ranch."

"You California folks are mighty queer, ain'tcha?" Great-uncle Rudd laughed. "Imagine that, Hoyt, they learn to stay on top of a horse at ridin' academies!"

Great-uncle Hoyt told him, "Rudd, it's 1929 now. The day of the horseless carriage has come. The horse has had his time in this country. This ain't the 1880's no more."

"Billy bedamned, Hoyt, sometimes I'm sorry that it ain't. In some ways that long-gone time was a better time."

"That's because we was young then, Rudd, and not so stove up," said Great-uncle Hoyt.

"And not under the thumb of a preacher's widow-woman who claims it's her last merciful mission on earth to live with the two of us." Great-uncle Rudd was frowning as he lowered himself onto the hay bale next to his brother.

Tuck changed the subject, perching himself on the last bale and leaving me standing up alone not far from Susie's stall. "Tell us about California back in 1880."

"Sure, me and Hoyt ain't doin' nothin' else now, jest waitin' for Carolina to put our lunch on the table and give us a call to come in and eat. You, Mo, don't jest stand there. Pull up that bucket over there, turn it over, and sit down on it. Ain't you never heard of a bucket seat?"

I saw the bucket he had in mind, brought it back, and then took up a mostly empty grain sack on the floor, put it on top for a cushion, and sat down facing the three of them. I'd sat on a bucket before, and I knew about the need for cushions on them.

Great-uncle Rudd grunted and began, "Well, sir, I'd been drivin' cattle up into Kansas for a number of years and had tired of that work, particularly after I'd been caught in five cattle stampedes in four years. Hoyt here knows how that can be. One minute all's peaceable as can be. Then somethin', mebbe nothin' more than a barkin' coyote, starts them cows a-runnin'. The first thing a man hears is some cattle bawlin', actin' restless; then all at once they're runnin' and poor cowboys is tryin' to stop 'em from runnin' so far that they run the beef off their bones and don't fetch so good a price at the market."

Hoyt said, "Yep, I been in a bad stampede once. Thinking about it now always puts me in mind of a poem that says somethin' like this:

Then came thunder in my ears
And over us surged the sea of steers!

"Purty words, ain't they, Tuck? I recall some more from that same poem. The poem was about a little old gal who got killed at the time:

For many a day the flowers have spread
A pall of petals over her head."

"He don't never recall the rest of the poem," said Great-uncle Rudd. "To go on with how I lost a piece of my ear way out in California, I made up my mind that I wasn't only tired of cowboy work, but it was gettin' altogether too unpleasant on the ranch, what with old Earl havin' truly got hisself married by that time to a ornery female. Not to mention that there was still six Quineys at home besides Earl. It got so I hated to come back to Santa Rosa County at all. So I rode over to the Puttiphut place and informed Clee that I'd like to try my luck at minin' gold out in California. So me and Clee, bein' footloose, fancy-free bachelors, got on our horses, him on white-maned Harley and me on Captain, and we lit out west by way of San Antone."

Tuck put in, "That's the way we drove here—through San Antonio."

Great-uncle Rudd ignored him. "We didn't stay long in that town, Clee and me. Why, I don't remember. We rode back east into Texas and turned our horses north toward the panhandle country. We left Texas ridin' north into New Mexico Territory.

"Lots of things happened to me and Clee as we swam them rivers and now and then picked up a week's pay workin' on ranches here and there. That's how we come to get to know old Billy the Kid pretty good—by workin' where he was also workin'."

I thought Tuck's eyes would pop out of his head. "You knew *him*?"

"For a time, until Clee crossed Billy by sayin' openly he didn't much favor Billy's singin' voice. Clee was partial to music, you see, and Billy's renderin' of tunes wasn't truly worth listenin' to. So me and Clee headed west again, and in Santa Fe we joined up with a party of folks headin' for California over the Old Spanish Trail, but we didn't stay too long with 'em. We left 'em and struck out for ourselves because one of the ladies, who was a widow two times over and two times Clee's age, had set her cap for him the first minute she clapped eyes on him. He didn't take much to her. Escapin' her, we wandered over most of Arizona Territory, seein' Bisbee and Prescott and other towns, but most of all we liked the town called Tombstone. That's where we got to know them Earp brothers, Virgil and Morgan and Wyatt, purty good too. We wasn't with 'em at that big gunfight at the O.K. Corral, though me and Clee woulda been on the Earp side if we was there. That fight didn't take place until we left Tombstone." Great-uncle Rudd took out his tobacco plug, bit some off, put it in his jaw, and started to chew.

Once he had the tobacco chewed up soft enough to talk, he went on. "Me and Clee Puttiphut left that interestin' town. We couldn't stay around Tombstone too long a time, because a faro dealer's wife fell madly in love with me. Because I liked the faro dealer and didn't want to have to shoot him, Clee and me rode out of Tombstone after sayin' farewell to the Earps and their tooth-jerker dentist friend, Doctor Holliday. We told them, naturally, in case they ever needed us to help them keep law and order, they could send word to Santa

Rosa County, Texas, where we was knowed to every man, woman, and child."

"You and Clee surely was well-knowed, Rudd," agreed Great-uncle Hoyt.

Great-uncle Rudd shot out a stream of brown juice to splatter on the barn floor, then said, "We betook ourselves down to Yuma, down by the Mexican border, and from there we swam our horses over the wide, brown Colorado River and into California. Then, in company with some others, we crossed the cruel-natured Mojave Desert over a high pass, into a big and purty valley with rock hills on all sides of it. There was farmers in it. It had a Mexican name I don't rightly recall."

"The San Bernardino Valley, Rudd," came from Hoyt.

"That's the right name for it, Hoyt. We didn't stay long in the little town of San Bernardino neither, 'cause Clee didn't like the saloons it had. They was too quiet to suit his nature. Not to mention too full of Yankees. California was plumb full of old blue-belly soldiers. We was hungry to talk to another Texan, and we heard from a bartender in San Bernardino that there was some minin' camps not far away that had lots of Southerners in 'em. So that's how we got to the Holcomb Valley. Holcomb Valley's the place I lost part of my left ear workin' in a gold mine. That valley had to be one of the most perilous places in the whole country at that time."

"Why?" I asked. I'd gone camping in Holcomb Valley once over the Easter holidays with my Girl Scout troop from Pasadena. Not one thing had happened there, except that I got a splinter in my finger and another girl got sunburned.

Great-uncle Rudd said, "Bear with me now, Mo, and you'll find out soon enough. It was because of all the wild critters in it. They was thick as bird shot in a shotgun shell. Deer and coyotes and opossums and skunks and rattlesnakes. But mostly it seemed to be bear there. There was even a valley nearby called Bear Valley. That ought to tell you what it was like up there in them hills. Them bears was black ones and grizzlies. A big, old grizzly has to be jest about the biggest thing there is and one of thc mcanest to boot.

"Me and Clee got ourselves jobs workin' in a mine for a man by the name of Jeb Borden. He hailed from Texas, too, and a nicer man nobody ever met. He had a mule that pulled the ore car out of his gold mine to the creek, so Borden could wash the dirt out of the gold. The mule was named Deuce. Deuce was jest full of the devil. He was a windsucker and a biscuit eater of the worst sort. When a man tried to saddle Deuce, he'd suck in a load of air, then let it out once the saddle was cinched. That way the saddle got so loose you'd have to cinch it all over again. As for his biscuit eatin', Deuce'd sneak right up into Borden's cabin when nobody was there and thieve the biscuits right out of the oven."

Pointing his finger at Great-uncle Rudd, my brother

exploded before I could, "No, sir! A mule can't open an oven door!"

"Tuck, them biscuits was made in a Dutch oven. Them kind of ovens go on top of the stove. A mule could get at them if he was careful about it, and Deuce surely was. To go on about Deuce, if you could get him saddled and bridled, he'd try to scrape his rider and his bedroll off against every tree or rock in the path. Deuce loved to flop down and try to roll in dirt or sand with full packs on his back. He didn't take to horses one bit. He tried every way he could to bite Borden's horses or to take a chunk out of Harley or Captain. And talk about kickin'! It was worth your life to get behind that mule. Yes, sir, they are a self-willed lot, mules is. If you don't watch 'em every minute, they'll get you. The only thing that'll make a mule behave is powerful cussin'.

"Old Clee Puttiphut could cuss to raise hair on a currycomb. He got along with Deuce fine from the start—better than I ever did. Finally that mule used to follow Clee around like a dog. Now and then he would chew away fondly at his shirt and other duds because of the salty sweat in them. A man works up a sweat in a mine, you see. Yep, Deuce took to Clee, and that was the only one he ever cared for. He didn't even cotton to Marinda, who was Borden's little girl and the pet of Holcomb Valley. She was a half orphan, motherless, so all of us looked out after her welfare. She was nine years old and a ray of sunshine—always laughin' and smilin'—a delight to behold. There was nothin' she liked better than to sit by the creek that run real close by the Borden mine and watch the trout play in the water. She was so tenderhearted that she wouldn't even take a fishin' pole with her, jest her old, blue-tick hound dog whose name I forgot by now.

"One hot summer day, while me and Clee was chipping away with pickaxes at the veins of solid gold in the mine and Mr. Borden was down in San Bernardino buyin' supplies, we heard her tick hound barkin' and barkin'. That wasn't nothin' new. He was a barkin' fool. But all at once the barkin' changed to a bayin'—and then a growlin' and a snarlin' and finally a god-awful howlin'.

"Hearin' all that, Clee and me looked at one another and put down our pickaxes. Course, we had six-guns in our belts like most other men, but now Clee grabbed up the shotgun we kept inside the mine. Out we ran toward that horrible howlin' sound. Old Deuce wasn't hitched up to the ore car jest at that moment. He was standin' outside the mine, waitin' for Clee to come out, leanin' against the rock wall eatin' a piece of towel Marinda had dropped over a huckleberry bush that mornin' to dry.

"Deuce lit right after us toward the howlin' too.

"An' now we heard screamin'. It was Marinda down by the creek. And she had to be in trouble to make that much noise. She wasn't a screamer by nature.

"Me and Clee, with Deuce hot at our heels, broke through the brush to the creek, and there we saw a truly horrible sight. There sat poor little Marinda on a rock in the middle of the creek. Her blue-tick hound was layin' dead on the far bank, its body busted to bits, while over it crouched the biggest grizzly bear I ever set eyes on. When the bear saw us, it reared up to what later proved to be nine feet in the air. That was somewhat biggern' Clee and me. It appeared to me that the two cubs behind the old ma bear was about our size. In a flash I seen what had happened. The bear had thought the barkin' hound was after one of her cubs and killed it.

"Clee, he was both brave and foolhardy. He fired the shotgun at the ma bear and he—" Great-uncle Rudd stopped to spit out some more tobacco juice and make us wait.

"What did he do?" demanded my brother.

"He missed, Tuck. He missed with both barrels. I shot the ma bear brute somewhere in its carcass, because she let out a growl of anger. In a flash she thundered past Marinda over the creek, splashin' water sky high, and flung herself on us, standin' side by side on the other bank. I shot her again. So did Clee with his six-gun, but we might as well have been shootin' at a passin' boxcar on a train. That ma grizzly took a swipe at Clee, knocking him clean off his feet into the air and right down into the creek water. The shotgun went flyin' through the air too, clear onto the other side, where it was useless to us."

"My gosh," breathed Tuck.

"Well, sir, that bear didn't pay no more heed right then to Clee. She gave all her attention to me. She gave me a swipe too, and after that when I was down, she sunk her fangs into my shoulder. Pullin' me with her teeth, she commenced to drag me into some nearby bushes. It appeared to me at that moment that I was goin' to be eaten by a bear.

"I went limp, playin' like I was dead, hopin' she had no appetite for a dead man and would leave me be—but not her. She let go for a bit, then started to claw my face and hands and shake me from front to back and from side to side while I prayed lots harder than I'd ever prayed in church. How that old bear snarled and growled, and finally she bit down into me again, with me lyin' flat on my face. Jest when I was certain that I was about to pass over the Great Divide and meet my Maker and be a bear's supper, I felt her wicked fangs let go of me suddenly.

"Raisin' my head from where I lay, I looked up and saw old Clee boldly beatin' at the bear with his Stetson hat. Now, of course, she went for him! She rared up again and raised her paw to give him another clout, when all at once Deuce came brayin' into the fight. You see, he jest couldn't bear to see his pal Clee attacked. Mules are mostly wary of bears, but not Deuce this time. He was somethin' to see, all right. He went past Clee at a run with his big mule ears laid back and them long teeth of his gnashin' and clashin' together. As he passed Clee, his withers knocked Clee out of the way.

"That old grizzly became Deuce's labor of the whole

week. He surely lit into her. First he bit the bear, then he whirled around lightnin' swift and delivered a kick in the bear's midsection that made her sit down hard on her sit-down. There's no kick in all of Mother Nature to match the kick of a mule in case you didn't know it.

"While the bear was down, Marinda came off that rock in the creek, picked up the shotgun and took out two shells she just happened to have in her apron pocket, loaded the piece, and let the grizzly have it with both barrels. Marinda didn't aim to miss. And she didn't neither. She killed that grizzly stone dead. Then she sat down after them cubs had run off and started to weep."

"Why?" asked my brother, grinning at me.

"She was weepin' for her blue-tick hound and for me. I was toothmarked from head to waist, and one of my arms was busted. But worse than that, according to her, my manly beauty was marred forever. One of the grizzly's long sharp claws had sliced off part of my left ear slick as a knife could as she tried to get a good purchase on me to drag me into the brush. In all the other pain that I was havin', I hadn't even taken note of the fact that part of my ear was gone. It was Marinda who noticed it. That hurt ear truly upset the tenderhearted little gal. Once I was healed of the dozen or so other wounds the bear had left, it didn't do no good at all for me to tell her that if that old grizzly had eaten any part of me the bear woulda been poisoned to death sure as could be.

"After that Mr. Borden sold the mine and went away, takin' Marinda with him and Deuce too. That mule couldn't be bought for any amount of money. Deuce never did a lick of work again neither. He was a mule hero, and he ate biscuits all the time from then on.

"Clee and me had made some money workin' for Borden, enough to get us home to Texas. On the way back we asked one another over and over again whether that grizzly truly ate part of my ear or not. We never could decide for certain."

I felt a little sick. I got up off the bucket, and at the same time Susie kicked the side of her stall and snorted, startling me. After I'd calmed down a bit, I said, "I don't really believe a word of that story. If a bear that size had bitten you, you would have been scarred all over. Your facc and hands aren't scarred one bit. And little girls don't have shotgun shells in their apron pockets."

"Nobody's holdin' you down, forcin' you to believe me," said Great-uncle Rudd.

"That's a darned good thing too." Leaving Tuck behind, I went back to the kitchen where Grandmother and Mrs. Hemmrich were sitting at the table looking at a little paper book together.

Mrs. Hemmrich was reading, pointing with a finger at a column in the book. "Susannah, you always plant by the moon. See what the almanac says. You plant onions in the sign of Aries, potatoes and peanuts in Taurus, but in Leo you should never plant anything. Plant cucumbers in Sagittarius." She looked up at me. "Yes, Merle, do you want a glass of lemonade?"

"No, thank you," I told her. Sitting down next to Grandmother, I said to her, "I just heard how Great-uncle Rudd was attacked by a grizzly bear back in 1880 out in California and lost his ear."

Grandmother smiled and said, "I hope you didn't swallow it."

"Oh, Grandmother!"

"Well, don't you fret. That yap of a brother of mine was not outside of Texas throughout the year of 1880. I know that for a fact. I know for a fact, too, that the only time he was ever in California was in the summer of 1881, and I was with him in San Diego just about every minute he was visiting your grandfather and me. Because I knew Rudd all too well, your grandfather and I had made a pact not to let him out of our sight. We nearly succeeded, too, except for one twenty-four-hour period."

She spoke to Mrs. Hemmrich, not to me. "It was because of what happened in that twenty-four hours that I cut my connections with him for so long. It was also the reason why we moved away from San Diego soon after we'd put Rudd on the train back to Texas."

"Oh, yes, I remember hearing about Rudd's visiting you, but I didn't know the particulars," Mrs. Hemmrich said. "Hoyt told me Rudd had visited you when I first came here to look after the two of them and trot myself half to death on their behalf. Lord, I rejoice that MacRae's as small as it is and Rudd is as old as he is and not frisky enough for much devilment anymore."

I asked, "What did he do in San Diego, Grandmother?"

She shook her head. "Nothing that I want to discuss,

Merle, or even think about. I haven't ever told your mother either. But if you want something to do now, you could tell your brother again not to believe everything he hears here in Texas." At her feet Brownie let out a whimpering sound.

That night when we went to bed in the Studebaker I got my first opportunity to talk to Graham alone. He'd stayed close to Hoyt and Rudd Quiney all day long, mostly out in the barn or walking around in the fields behind the house while I'd been inside with the women.

I sat in the back seat with Brownie on my lap and leaned over the front seat to tell him what Grandmother had said about Great-uncle Rudd's being nowhere near California in 1880 and about not believing everything he was told in Texas.

The words came from my brother in a sleepy mumble. "I don't really believe most of what Rudd says for a minute. How dumb does Grandma think I am, anyhow? I like to hear the old guy's whoppers, that's all. The one about the bear was okay, and I liked the one about the mule, but the knitting needle and Avarilla Arrowwood is still my favorite. And you can tell Grandma something for me, too, if you dare." He sounded wide-awake now.

"What's that?"

"Something funny Great-uncle Rudd said he told to a lady back in Oklahoma Territory in 1873 because she talked all the time. He said, 'Oh, go lay a egg and get something for your cackle.' "

I twitched, and Brownie got down off my lap for the

car seat. "That sounds just like Great-uncle Rudd," I flared at my brother. "You tell Grandmother that! I'm not going to tell her. I like her a lot better than I do Great-uncle Rudd, let me tell you. She isn't a big old liar for one thing. If you say that to any lady, and Mom hears about it, she'll wash out your mouth with soap after she skins you alive. And I'll help hold you down while she does it. I'll ask Grandmother to help hold you, too. The more I see of her out here the more I like her. Remember, she never went to regular school the way we do. I've been thinking about that. We're lucky to have a school to go to. Just look at our great-uncles who can't read and write. That's awful. Think of what their lives might have been like if they could have."

"I'll bet Great-uncle Rudd would still tell whoppers," my brother answered.

I said, "Maybe so, but they'd be better ones, I'll bet."

7
Them Old Red Dundalks

"There are only three more days to stay here now, dog," I told Brownie softly the next morning, as she lay sprawled over me licking my face.

Before "Tuck" was awake to argue with me again, I was out of the car in my kimono carrying Grandmother's dog. I was scared Brownie might run off behind the house or across the road into thc fields, and I remembered what Dad had said about a coyote's getting the dog. As for "Tuck," I figured that the noise I made shutting the car door would wake him up.

I was up so early this morning that only Mrs. Hemmrich was around. She was just closing the oven of the black iron stove after she'd put the breakfast biscuits inside. "Oh, good morning, Merle," she said, as I set Brownie down. "How did you sleep?"

"All right, but I don't think Brownie is resting very well out there in the car with me. She's used to being with Grandmother all the time. Can't she stay in the house with her tonight?"

The housekeeper shook her head. "It's never been our custom to keep dogs inside this house. I've been afraid to give in to the idea for fear of having hound dogs all over the place. Hoyt likes them well enough, even if we don't have one. You might ask him for his permission."

I said over the loud noises of Brownie's lapping water from the bowl set out for her, "I shouldn't ask him. Grandmother ought to. It's her dog, not mine, Mrs. Hemmrich."

"She won't, child. I doubt if she'd ask either one of her brothers for a favor. After all, she's never written them in all these years she's been corresponding with me. She could have enclosed a letter now and then for them, but she never did. It isn't as if I couldn't have read it to them, and they could have had me write back to her. You see, Merle, there's some bad feelings on both sides—on all three sides is a better way to put it."

I said, "But Great-uncle Hoyt really seemed glad to have her come here!"

"He did. He doesn't hold grudges the way Rudd does, or the way she does for that matter." Mrs. Hemmrich shook her head. Her long cotton apron was lavender and pink with little blue flowers on it today. She looked pretty in it, like a small gray bird.

This three-way business was too much for me to take in all at once. It seemed to me that the three old people were acting as badly as Graham and I did toward each other at times. It was wrong. They were too old for such behavior.

"Where is everybody anyway?" I asked.

"Your mother and grandmother haven't come down yet, but Hoyt and Rudd are out in the barn. They've had their coffee already." She smiled at me. "Why don't you take some morning coffee up to your mother and Susannah now?"

I said, "Sure, they'd like that. I'll take Brownie with me, and while I'm upstairs I'll get dressed." All of our suitcases were in the guest room.

As she was pouring coffee from the big blue-and-white speckled pot on the stove top, Mrs. Hemmrich told me, "Put on your best bib and tucker, Miss Tucker. It's Sunday morning, and we'll be going to church. Susannah said last night she wants to go. She wants to show some of the people in these parts that all of the Quineys aren't savages and heathens."

"Sunday!" I'd lost track of thc days. Thcn a ncw idca came to me. "But you haven't got a buggy anymore. How'll we get there?"

"We'll be going with the couple across the road. The church isn't far from here, only a couple miles down the road toward Dallas. We can all pile into their wagon."

I said, "Wagon?" I'd expected a buggy, but not a wagon.

"Yes. It's their go-to-meeting wagon, not the one they use to carry their cotton to the gin."

I said, "Oh?" as I took a tray with a glass of milk for me and two cups of black coffee on it. Then a new idea came to me. "Do my great-uncles go to church too?"

"No, dear." She laughed. "I've tried for years to get them there, just so they can be exposed to religion now and then. Sometimes I think Hoyt might go, but Rudd always talks him out of it."

Then I asked, "Do you know why Great-uncle Rudd is the way he is, Mrs. Hemmrich?"

She nodded firmly. "Oh, yes. Years ago Susannah told me Rudd was born during the eclipse of the sun. Everything went dark all over Texas for five minutes before Rudd Quiney arrived and for five minutes afterwards."

"Gosh!" This was interesting information.

"Well, naturally, after I'd learned that fact about him and inasmuch as I already had his birthday and year, I was able to sum up the man. A book gave me the time of the eclipse that day. With all this I went ahead and made a horoscope for him. It was something! You see, he was born in October, in the sign of Libra, the Scales. That gives him his charm as a storyteller. His moon is in Aries and his ascendant in Scorpio. Aries is the sign of the battering ram and Scorpio of the stinging scorpion. Don't you see now?"

I know I must have been staring at her, absolutely rooted to the spot by the explanation she'd given me. She laughed and told me, "Well, that satisfies me. Take the coffee up before it gets cold. I'll open the stairway door for you and the dog."

Halfway up the steps, I heard her calling me, so I stopped. "Merle, please tell your mother that according to the almanac, the moon went into Virgo early this morning, so her wrist should improve rapidly now. You all should be able to get on the road again by Wednesday morning if she keeps on soaking her wrist, even if it's going to rain tomorrow and Tuesday."

"Is it going to?" I asked, as Brownie went scrambling past me up the steep stairs.

"Oh, yes, it may be hot as blue and red blazes right now, but it will rain."

"Did the almanac tell you that?" I remembered that the almanac said all sorts of things about when to plant and the weather.

"It didn't have to. Hoyt told me last night. He says his broken shoulder is aching right now. It never fails to rain when Hoyt aches somewhere."

"Brownie!" That was Grandmother's voice, letting me know that she was awake.

So was Mom, sitting up in the other little bed.

As I set the tray down, I told them, "Mrs. Hemmrich sent me up here." Brownie was on top of the patchwork quilt on Grandmother's bed, whining and being petted. "She said for me to get dressed up, because we're going to church with some neighbors."

"I can't," came from Mom, as she reached with her good arm for the coffee on the table between the two beds. "I'm going to eat breakfast, take some more aspirin, and soak my wrist."

"Mom, Mrs. Hemmrich says we'll be able to leave by Wednesday."

"Lordy, I hope she's right, Merle. I feel better. I even had a good night's sleep last night. But I feel as if I'm in a prison here—or a hospital. I've always thought a hospital was worse than a prison."

Grandmother was patting her dog, not even seeming interested in her coffee. She said, "Floy, I'm sorry about your wrist, but in a way I'm glad it happened where it did. Now please hear me out and don't get angry." She paused, looking over at Mom. "You know, my dears, if that bridge hadn't washed out and you hadn't had to use the crank, we would never have come here to MacRae. It was truly the finger of fate. I was brought here by fate to see Hoyt and Rudd once more. I was quite sure of it when you had that accident. I'm convinced by now. I was brought here to make peace with my brothers. I dreamed last night that we were children together down home on the ranch in Santa Rosa County. I think that my being here ties up a loose end at last. I am sorry I treated them badly by not writing to them through Carolina for all these years. I could have. She and I have talked about it. Carolina is a saint. She has made me see the light more clearly than I ever would have seen it by myself."

Mom asked after a swallow of coffee, "Do you think Rudd and Hoyt see it that way, too?"

"I suspect that Hoyt does. Hoyt understands a lot of things he doesn't talk about. He understands Rudd very well and is very kind to him. I know that I have to forgive Rudd."

"What do you have to forgive him for, Mother?" Mom asked.

"I don't wish to discuss that, Floy. Let me say only that the name of Rudd Quiney is not unknown to the police department out in San Diego."

"My, oh my!" Mom took another sip, then chuckled.

I waited to hear what Grandmother would add and so did Mom, but that was all that was said. After that Grandmother started in on her coffee too.

"Okay, get dressed, Merle," Mom told me, "and then please tell your brother about going to church with you. I suppose it's going to be hot. You'd better put on one of the white linen dresses I bought you to wear in New Orleans. Get out the white satin bow for your hair."

A little later, all dressed up, I went out to the car to tell my brother what Mom had said. He was outside the car in his pajamas, and he wasn't alone. Great-uncle Rudd was with him. Together they were pushing the mailbox off the car into an upright position.

"Holy snakes, little Mo!" exploded my Great-uncle. "You look like you're either gettin' married or buried, all duded up in white. Don't you go near the mare in the barn lookin' like a ghost or you'll spook her. Horses don't like to see a lot of black or white all at one time."

Oh, but he could make a girl angry! I said, "We're going to church, Grandmother and Mrs. Hemmrich and me. I came out to tell my brother to get dressed to go with us."

Graham said, "I don't aim to. Tell Mom I don't want to get all duded up for church. I'm going to spend the morning out in the barn, and then Great-uncle Rudd's going to show me where he keeps his whiskey still. It's a secret."

Quick as a flash, Rudd asked me, "Mo, don't you hanker to see it too?"

In a way I did and in a way I didn't. I said, "Are you a bootlegger?"

"Nope, Mo, I don't sell it to nobody. I drink it all up myself."

"But you could go to jail all the same for just making it, couldn't you?"

"So they say."

I shook my head. "No, I don't want to see your still. That way if the police come to get you while we're here and ask me where your still is, I really won't know, will I?" I added, "I surely don't want to have the police come here, and I don't think Mrs. Hemmrich or Great-uncle Hoyt want that either. It would be awful if the police took down their names and put them into jail, wouldn't it?" That should fix him. It would make him think of his crimes in San Diego.

But he didn't even blink, and he didn't say anything. My brother did, though. He bragged, "If the police come here, even if they're like those old sheriffs in New Mexico Territory you told me about and torture me, I won't tell them where the still is hidden."

My, but living in MacRae with Rudd had certainly affected all of us. Graham had become Tuck and was talking back to everybody, Grandmother had got so mellow and gentle that she wasn't the same person she'd been in Pasadena, and I was growing angrier every minute of every day. The only one who hadn't changed so far was Mom, and she'd kept to her room. I thought the sooner we left MacRae the better. I said to Graham, "I'm not going to say one word of what you've been saying to Mom. I'm going to tell her that you've got a stomachache and don't feel up to going to church. She feels sick enough without your making her feel worse." Mom did feel better, but she wasn't well enough yet in my estimation to swat Graham the way he ought to be swatted.

Great-uncle Rudd did a terrible thing then. He made that shame-on-you gesture with his fingers, and he dared to say, "You'll be tellin' a lie to your ma, Mo."

I couldn't think of anything to say to him that would be bad enough, so I turned around and ran back to the house.

During breakfast, after Graham had dressed, I didn't say much at all. Mom talked to Mrs. Hemmrich and Great-uncle Hoyt, and Grandmother told Graham three times, if his stomach hurt him, not to gobble so many hot biscuits.

He glared at me after he'd had to put the fourth one back into the basket that was passed around the table. That served him right. When nobody was looking, I stuck my tongue out at him as I ate my fourth biscuit.

I kept marveling at Grandmother most of all, though. She was trying to be pleasant to her brother Rudd, asking him how he slept and if he thought it would rain too, and what he thought of President Herbert Hoover.

He certainly didn't try to be pleasant to her in return. He went on shoving biscuits and bacon and eggs into his mouth with the busiest knife and fork I'd ever seen. He never looked at her. When he was finished, though, he pushed his plate away and, while Hoyt was still eating his second egg, said, "As for all them things you been pesterin' me about, Pike, I didn't sleep good because Hoyt snores so bad. Hoyt's shoulder says it'll rain even if my arthuritis in my right knee ain't totally convinced yet. I been a Democrat all my life, so naturally I think that Republican President Hoover is ruinin' the country. And let me tell you one thing more—we're in for hard times in the country purty soon. We've had good times too long. Too many folks is spendin' too much money for things they don't have no use for, like automobiles." He squinted up at the ceiling. "There are some stories I could tell you about hard times. . . ."

"There certainly are, Rudd," came from Carolina Hemmrich, "but we have to hurry now to get to church. The stories will have to wait."

"They will, I imagine. Say a prayer there for me and Hoyt, Carolina."

"I always do. How else do you suppose you've managed to survive all these years, Rudd?" Mrs. Hemmrich was out of the chair now, reaching for her own dishes.

Grandmother and I picked up ours and Mom's and took them to the kitchen right after her. Then Mom got settled in the kitchen with her wrist in hot water again, with Brownie crouching like a lion under the table nearby. The wagon was waiting out front when Grandmother and Mrs. Hemmrich, who both carried parasols, were ready to go. The wagon had three seats in it, one behind another, and was painted very dark green with yellow wheel spokes. The neighbor couple were a little bit younger than Grandmother. Mrs. Hemmrich introduced us to them, and then Mr. Gress helped both of us into the wagon and off we went to church behind a pair of strange-looking, long-eared horses I learned were mules.

It was a nice, little, white Methodist church. I knew most of the hymns and felt pretty much at home. Everyone acted surprised to meet Rudd and Hoyt Quiney's sister and her granddaughter from all the way out in California.

The preacher's wife seemed to be an old friend of Mrs. Hemmrich's. After church, while I was standing outside with Grandmother under her parasol, I heard this lady talking. "Carolina, how are you doing, ministering to those two heathen men?"

"You mean Rudd, mostly. He's no better. I found the Comanche Indians more gracious, even if I never did get used to seeing men with their hair in long braids and wearing earrings." She laughed, nodded good-bye, and went off to the wagon with the Gresses and the two of us.

As she sat down, she said to Grandmother, "Susannah, I do hope Floy remembered to put the chicken in to roast at ten minutes to twelve, so we can eat dinner by two thirty."

"Carolina, stop worrying. Floy will remember."

"Hoyt and Rudd will expect their dinner right on the dot. They're even worse about that on Sunday."

What I'd heard about the Indians interested me more than my great-uncles, so I asked, "Did Comanche men really wear jewelry?"

"Oh my, yes, they did. Necklaces and beads and fur trimmings and silver gewgaws. In the old days a Comanche brave was a sight to see. The Comanches are a most interesting tribe. They are very religious. They believe that a Comanche is reborn again and again after he dies. He always returns as a Comanche, however, not as anyone in any other tribe and not as a white man, let me assure you. They are a very proud lot. It was not an easy task for a missionary—trying to convert a Comanche Indian."

And then Mrs. Hemmrich went on talking to Grandmother about the difficulties her husband had being a missionary on a reservation. Next they talked about churches they'd both gone to. Because I was bored with listening to that, I looked out over the flat country and the cotton fields and then the backs of the mules as they swished flies away with their tails. It was so hot my knees stuck together and the palms of my hands sweated. Even if it meant coming back to Great-uncle Rudd and a brother who was turning into somebody I wasn't sure I wanted to know anymore, it would be nice to get back to the cool, little house in MacRae.

Mom hadn't forgotten about the chicken. We had a wonderful dinner of roast hen, gravy, potatoes, corn, greens, rhubarb, and strawberry-preserve pie. Afterwards Mrs. Hemmrich said she was so stuffed all she wanted to do was sit and rock out on the veranda. The dishes could wait. So we took out enough chairs for everybody, and all of us went out onto the veranda to sit down. Brownie came too and lay down at Grandmother's feet with her eyes on the road, which was empty as far as you looked in any direction. The horn chairs weren't rockers. All the same Great-uncle Rudd seemed to be able to loll in his. I figured he'd shown his still to Graham and probably drunk something wherever it was. He hadn't asked for any arthritis medicine after dinner.

I watched him squinting up at the sky. "Hoyt," he said, "do you still say we're goin' to have some rain?"

"Yep, Rudd, I do. There's for certain goin' to be a change in the weather."

There was a long silence, and then I broke it. "Great-uncle Rudd, Mrs. Hemmrich said you were born in an eclipse of the sun."

"I was indeed, Mo, or so I was told. I don't remember it myself, bein' only a baby at the time."

"You were born in one, Rudd," came from Grandmother.

"I guess I got to take your word on that, Susie," he said. "Eclipses is queer things to be in. First thing you know, it gets dark, then colder, and the wind dies down. And you think it's dusk come at high noon. Whereas some folks get scared, the animals get flustered. The chickens go to their roostin' places, and because the cows think it's milkin' time, they start for the barn to be milked. And then all the animals get a big surprise, because it gets bright sunshine again."

"Rudd, eclipses are better'n blizzards. They don't ever endure for long," said Great-uncle Hoyt.

"A danged sight better. Yes, sir, I was born in a eclipse, but Carolina here was born durin' a blizzard, wasn't you? But because she was a baby then too, she wouldn't know as much as I do about blizzards."

"Oh, my! I forgot the dishes!" Mrs. Hemmrich's words surprised me. She got up right after she'd spoken. She'd been the one who suggested leaving the dishes and sitting out on the veranda. Now she was through the screen door, heading for the kitchen, before anyone could stop her.

Great-uncle Rudd waited until the screen door clicked shut, then said, "I recall one blizzard in partic'lar. Billy bedamned, it's long gone by, but I remember it like it was yesterday. It was the winter of 1878—January, it was—and that was when I lost part of my left ear. It was all because of them danged Red Dundalks."

"What are Red Dundalks?" Mom asked.

"Cows, Floy. A breed of red cows from Scotland. Me and Clee Puttiphut was workin' them days for a rancher up near the border of Oklahoma Territory. He brung them over from Scotland to try out in Texas."

"*Clee Puttiphut*!" exploded Grandmother. "Red Dundalk cows!" She got up too, grabbed Brownie, and went through the screen door.

Great-uncle Hoyt said, "It appears to me that Carolina's goin' to have some help with them dinner dishes. Are you goin' too, Floy?"

"No, Uncle Hoyt. I'm comfortable out here, thank

you. And with my wrist the way it is, I wouldn't be much good drying dishes." Mom was rocking, fanning herself with a piece of palm leaf that had been put down on the veranda railing. "My, but those yellow roses are pretty, and so fragrant," she murmured.

"That's the Texas flower," said Hoyt.

"But I thought bluebonnets were," Mom said.

"They both are," answered Great-uncle Rudd, "but none of them could hold a candle for color to them Red Dundalks that yellow-bearded Englishman Mr. Morehouse brung over. They was purty cows all right, the purtiest I had ever set eyes on. They was deep, dark red all over, such a nice red you never saw on a cow. Meat to the hocks too—good beef stock. The only thing wrong with 'em was that they was loco."

"I know that word. It means crazy," commented my brother. "The cowboys in the pictures are always calling somebody loco."

"Well, Tuck, them Red Dundalks was truly loco. They purely enjoyed gettin' stuck in bog holes and drownin' in flooded rivers and walkin' over cliffs. My horse, Captain, knew it, and Clee's horse, Harley, knew it, because they had horse sense, but old Mr. Morehouse, who owned them fancy cows, never did. He wouldn't believe they was loco, though he believed people could be. He wouldn't believe me when I told him in September that there was a bad winter comin' along. Me and Clee, we knowed it. You tell 'em, Hoyt, how come we knowed that."

Great-uncle Hoyt nodded. "This is gospel, folks. A

man can tell a bad winter's due by a number of things. That fall was remembered for years, because ranches had never seen cow hair and horsehair grow so thick. What's more, the fur on the bottom of a jackrabbit's foot was thicker too, and the hoofs of cows busted off earlier than usual. Them was bad-weather signs, all of 'em."

"There was more," said Rudd. "The grass up on Mr. Morehouse's ranch that summer was the darkest green I ever set eyes on, and to boot there was lots more thunder late that fall than usual. Me and Clee and them other cowboys knowed we was in for a bad time, because we had the care of them loco Dundalks. A self-respectin' old Texas longhorn knows when a blue norther of a storm's on the way before it comes. A steer will look to the north and do some bawlin' and then turn around with his tail to the storm.

"We was plenty worried about them fancy cows from Scotland, though. What were they goin' to do when they met their first norther? When the first big snow came, we learned fast enough. We was right about them cows. Right off, them old Red Dundalks started movin' around over the countryside instead of standin' still like a longhorn. They began runnin' in all directions—every which way. Let me tell you, it was hard work for all us cowboys ridin' around herdin' all them loco brutes together to get 'em to shelter on their home range. It took the best part of three days.

"Well, sir, I thought I was near froze in the cold before we got some of them loco cows together to drive them to a shelter we knowed of. And then the storm got worse than ever. That there snow had begun first comin' down gentlelike but thick. Straight down out of the sky it came. Them first flakes was big ones, but wet ones. Some of 'em lasted long enough on a glove for a man who had the time to make out the purty picture it made. But then all of a sudden it got colder, and that north wind out of the Indian Nations started up a howlin' and screamin'. Them snowflakes got littler and littler and after a time stung a man or horse or cow like someone was jabbing him with needles."

"Knitting needles?" asked my brother with a smile.

"No, darnin' needles, Tuck. And it wasn't no laughin' matter. All the same you're right on one point. My losin' my ear did have to do with knittin'. But this time it wasn't that Arrowwood gal in Fort Worth. It was your Grandma Susie's knittin'. It was all her fault I lost my ear part."

I exploded, "Grandmother's fault?"

"Mo, you jest listen and see. Now we surely had our troubles with them red cows. Ever' time we'd get 'em headed in the right direction in spite of the ragin' blizzard, two or three of the loco brutes'd run off to the side of the trail. Finally, it got so hard to see that the only way I knowed Captain was still there was because I could feel him with my knees under me. Them danged Red Dundalks, in spite of our yellin' and cussin' at them and ridin' back and forth, was bound and determined to go each his own way.

"I was sure that I was not only blue with the cold

but jest as sure that my tobacco plug had froze solid inside my pocket. That worried me some, the fact that I might not have any good chewin' tobacco anymore. Jest to satisfy my curiosity about it, I felt for the plug. That's when I felt that queer knitted thing next to where the plug was. It was a thing Susie had sent me for Christmas. I was usin' it as a chest protector, but truly it was a cap. It had a hole in it for a man's face to show out of, but everywhere else his head was covered up, and it buttoned under his chin. It surely had been a strange-lookin' danged thing, but out of lovin' brotherly sentiment I'd hung onto it. Old Mr. Morehouse had told me what it was called. He said it was a balaclava helmet, and it was supposed to keep a man's skull warm. So I took off my hat and pulled that there helmet on somehow, though in all that wind and snow while ridin' a horse and chasin' after a strayed steer and jugglin' a big Stetson hat it wasn't easy. I'd never even tried the helmet on for size, because I surely hated the color. You see, it was a pale baby blue.

"Well, sir, that was a mistake on my part, my never having put on that thing first so I could get a good look at it with my head inside it. After I put it on, I put the Stetson back on top of it, not carin' if it was baby color or not.

"It got colder then and the work harder, because them Red Dundalks that hadn't run off to the right or left kept droppin' in their tracks givin' up and freezin' to death. Me and Clee couldn't do a thing for 'em, excepting to get down off Captain and Harley and hoist a half-dead calf apiece up over our saddles, remount, and go on again drivin' ahead of us what was left of the herd.

"Finally, we reached where we was headed for on the range and got fifty or so of them cows to a place where they could weather out the blizzard. There was a shack there that Mr. Morehouse kept to house his cowboys in better weather when they were checkin' to see that his barbed-wire fences wasn't cut by beef rustlers."

My brother interrupted. "Mo, tell him that we know all about rustlers from the picture shows."

"We know!" That was all I'd say.

Great-uncle Rudd went on. "That's good. It saves my breath explainin' about them. Well, there was a little mirror for shavin' in that shack, and once we'd got a fire goin' good in the stove in it and thawed ourselves out a bit, we started takin' off our duds. I happened to be lookin' into that mirror when I took off my hat, preparin' to take off the knit helmet, too, which by this time was cruelly bindin' my scalp and around my chin.

"*And then what did I see*? It made me yelp, you bet."

"What?" Graham asked, grinning again.

"I seen all them knots and lumps and holes in that there helmet Susie had knit for me. You never saw nothin' like that helmet in your life. She'd made so many mistakes droppin' stitches it looked more like blue lace than knittin'. Yarn stuck out every which way like I had whiskers on top of my head. But that wasn't the worst part of the thing. The worst knittin' of all was on the left side of the danged helmet where wool shoulda been coverin' my ear. A bee musta bit Susie while she was knittin' on that part, and she musta dropped the needles. There was a hole down there big enough for half of my left ear to stick out through.

"It had stuck out at one time—but no more! That part of my ear had froze solid somewhere along the way to the shack and dropped off into the snow. Gone forever, but not forgotten! There wasn't no use goin' back to look for it to give it a church-type burial. Me and Clee would never find it."

I heard Mom giggling. She said, "Well, that's quite a story, Uncle Rudd, but I happen to know that my mother can't knit at all. She crochets sometimes and she embroiders, but she doesn't knit."

"Yes, ma'am, that's what I jest said. She can't knit! Even before she took to wearin' the short skirts you females wear nowadays, she couldn't knit worth a dang."

I'd moved to the rocker Grandmother had left. Rocking back and forth because I was furious, I said, "I don't believe that there are any Red Dundalk cows either."

"Go look 'em up in that book of Carolina's," said Great-uncle Hoyt.

"I'm going to—right away." I couldn't help doing what I did then. I rubbed the first finger of my right hand over the first finger of the left, letting Great-uncle Rudd know just what I thought of his latest story. And he'd dare to do that to me when I fibbed to Mom that Graham had a stomachache.

The old man nodded at me, smiled, and then all at

once closed his right eye in a great big, very slow wink.

I said to him, "Someday before we go you'll have to tell Mom about Avarilla Arrowwood's knitting too. I think that's the best story you've told yet about how you lost your ear."

"I'm glad you liked it, Mo."

"Yes, it's quite a lot longer than this one too," said my brother.

"Why are you complainin' about that, Tuck? Didn't I already tell you today while them women was off at church about how I lost that piece of me in a duel with bullwhips while visitin' the town of Laredo with Clee Puttiphut back in 1872? Did you fancy hearing how the tip of my ear was flicked off by that there Mexican's bullwhip better than what I jest told you?"

"Yes, I guess I did, but I still like the one Mo likes best of all."

As Mom chuckled and bent down to fondle Brownie's ears, she said, "I didn't know there was so much entertainment here in MacRae. I'd been missing the radio and picture shows, but you don't seem to need them, do you?"

"Nope, Floy, we don't," agreed Great-uncle Hoyt. "Rudd and me, we never seen a picture show or listened to a radio machine." He turned his head to me. "Mo, ain't you goin' to look up them Red Dundalks in that there bunch of books she's got, that 'cyclopedium?"

I asked, "Would there be any real use in my doing that?"

"Not truly, Mo, but there's some interestin' stuff in there about cows. Lots of pictures."

I got up and went over to my brother and whispered into his ear, "Can I see you over there?" I pointed to the veranda railing on the other side. When he came over, I asked, "What about the bullwhip story? Could it have been true?"

"I'm sure it wasn't. He told it to me down by his still. Afterwards I asked Great-uncle Hoyt about bull-whips, and he said Rudd didn't know one end of a bullwhip from another and had only been to Laredo one time. Hoyt was there with him and Earl back in 1870, not 1872 at all. Rudd was fourteen years old that year."

This was enough for me. It was too much! I left the veranda, slamming the screen door behind me just the way Grandmother had. I was glad she hadn't heard that story about her knitting. He'd meant to insult her —and she was trying to forgive him!

8

Ransom—or Else

Helping dry the dishes out in the kitchen, I told Grandmother and Mrs. Hemmrich, "Great-uncle Rudd told two stories today. I heard one of them, the one about a blizzard, some red cows that weren't real, and a cap you knitted for him. Mom caught him out. She said you couldn't knit at all, Grandmother. The other story he told was to Graham. It was about a duel Rudd fought with bullwhips when he was sixteen years old."

The housekeeper put a platter down into a lower cupboard, straightened up, and said, "I remember having heard both of those dreadful tales. I was afraid when I heard that word *blizzard* that I'd have to hear one of them again. Naturally, neither of them is true. Is your mother still out on the veranda?"

"Yes, she is. Great-uncle Rudd was telling her that he thinks ladies' skirts are too short these days."

"Oh, Rudd does," agreed Mrs. Hemmrich. "He says that he never wanted to have to live long enough to see a woman's ankles, let alone her knees. He liked it better back before 1900 when we wore long skirts that dragged in the dust and mud and wore high-top shoes and corsets that cut us in two." She shook her head. "If men only knew or cared what ladies suffered then, particularly in hot weather. Or how we slaved in those heavy, awkward clothes over hot stoves. We had to look like ladies and work like animals."

"Well, Carolina, that day is gone to some extent." Grandmother nodded over the cup she was wiping. "My Floy has a washing machine with a wringer on top of it, and when we get home to California, she's going to throw out her old icebox and buy something called a refrigerator."

"A refrigerator? What's that?" asked Mrs. Hemmrich.

"Good gracious, haven't you heard about them here yet? Well, it's a new machine that acts like an icebox. It keeps food fresh, but it makes ice too."

"What will they think of next!" Mrs. Hemmrich looked shocked.

"Who knows what someone will think of next?" Grandmother said. "My daughter Floy surely didn't grow up the way I did on the Quiney home ranch. The motorcar wasn't invented then. And we women had long hair and long skirts and never thought of anything but marrying the boy on the ranch to the east or the west of ours. Why—Floy even worked as a secretary for her husband before she married him. She votes in the elections. John doesn't tell her how to vote either. He doesn't dare to. She bobbed her hair and learned how to drive the automobile she bought with her own money. And now she aims to get an all-steel refrigerator, even if they do cost over $200."

"Gracious, that's higher than a cat's back, isn't it, Susannah?"

"Yes, but as Floy says, it will be worth it not to have to stay home to meet the iceman when he comes every week, and there won't be all that mess when he drips water from the ice all over the kitchen floor."

Mrs. Hemmrich shook her head and said, "I guess we can get along all right with the old box here. Rudd and Hoyt wouldn't take at all to my asking them for a refrigerator. They're against anything modern."

It made me feel better to add, "Billy bedamned, they sure are!"

"Well, I'm not," vowed Grandmother. "I'm for progress, and I'm proud as can be of Floy, though when she first began to drive I had some moments of doubt. Floy is as modern as a women can be—up-to-the-minute in just about everything. Speaking of your mother, Merle, is she going upstairs to lie down before Rudd starts in on his second Sunday afternoon lie?"

"She didn't say that she was, Grandmother. She heard all of that story about the blizzard, and at the end she laughed. She liked it, it seemed to me. She was still sitting out there when I came in here."

"Merle," said Mrs. Hemmrich, "will you go back there with a tray of lemonade glasses to save me the trip?"

After I nodded, she went out onto the back porch where the icebox was to get the big pitcher of lemonade I'd squeezed the lemons for.

I asked Grandmother, "Do you want me to tell Mom you think she ought to rest? Maybe she's too polite to walk away from Great-uncle Rudd's lies."

"Let her do as she pleases. We both know she's been bored here. Perhaps she finds my brothers entertaining. I'll stay out here with Carolina and have a cup of weariness tea with her. Then I can copy down her recipes for pickles and fried-apple pie."

Weariness tea? That was new to me. When Mrs. Hemmrich was back with the pitcher and was pouring lemonade into five glasses, I asked, "What's in weariness tea?"

"Dandelions, yarrow, and nettles, Merle. It strengthens a person wonderfully well. I think your grandmother needs it now. Forgiving your Great-uncle Rudd and not sassing him back for his bad manners takes a lot out of a body."

"That's true." I took the tray and said, "That is gospel truth!"

"That sounds like Hoyt!" And Mrs. Hemmrich laughed.

They were on the veranda exactly as I'd left them except for my brother and Brownie. He was rocking in the chair I'd left, with the dog in his arms.

Great-uncle Hoyt was talking to Mom. "No, Floy, I wasn't never a Texas Ranger. I spent all of my days as a cowboy and a bronc snapper, a horsebreaker. That's why I'm so stove up. I musta busted every bone in my body at least one time. After Rudd's little Ruby Nell died and somebody ridin' past the ranch I was workin' at told me the sorry news, I come down to find my brother. And so I did find him. Him and me worked as cowboys together for a spell, and then I got into a poker game in Dallas and won me this here little home. So we moved in, him and me, and tried to live here for a spell as bachelors. But my cookin' didn't suit him and his didn't suit me, so we asked Carolina Hemmrich to come cook for the pair of us. She don't do so poorly at it as Rudd claims she does."

I gasped. Mrs. Hemmrich was a wonderful cook!

Rudd said to Mom, "I swear sometimes Carolina boils the dishrag with the soup." Though he was talking to Mom, he was looking at the tray I was carrying. It was a suspicious look he gave the lemonade, I thought.

"It's only lemonade," I told him. I gave Mom the first glass, being polite.

He said, "At first glance I'd had hopes it was my arthuritis medicine. I'd like a taste of that right now. My knees pain me from all this sittin'." I gave him a glass, and he took it. Then he turned to Mom and said, "No, Hoyt wasn't no Texas Ranger, but I used to be. I can tell you a story about my days as one of them famous lawmen that'll make your eyes hang out on your shirtfront. I lost part of my ear in the service of them noble Texas Rangers."

I heard my brother snort, but I didn't look at him. I looked at Mom, rocking quietly in her chair. She hadn't gone to church, but she'd dressed up all the same. I thought she looked nice in her pale-green georgette dress. It went well with her short, marcelled red hair. She was smiling as she held her lemonade in her good hand and said, "I think it would be interesting to hear about your life with the Texas Rangers, Uncle Rudd."

"You bet it is, Floy. As soon as your little gal stops sashayin' around with that lemonade, I'll start on it. Billy bedamned, it was back in 1872. That's long gone by."

As I added and subtracted dates in my head, wishing I had pencil and paper, Graham said, "But you remember it like it was yesterday?"

"That's right, Tuck." Rudd gave me a look as I put the tray down by my chair and picked up the last glass.

"I'm through sashayin'," I told him. "And Grandmother said you were born in 1856, so that would make you sixteen years old then."

"Maybe it was a slightly later time, at that, Mo. I don't always remember the exact year when things happened in my life. But sixteen was a man in Texas in them years, let me tell you. Well, sir, I'd enlisted for twelve months in the Texas Rangers. Like every other one of them men, I was a stranger to fear and had wonderful determination. I was also a dead shot. I furnished my own horse, Captain, and my own rifle and Colt six-shot revolver. The Rangers gave me my grub and one dollar a day, a set of handcuffs, and a list of wrongdoers in the state of Texas."

"A list of men wanted—of criminals," explained Hoyt.

"That's so. After that, they sent me out to find them wanted men and bring 'em back so they could be judged and hung. So I rode about west Texas in company with Captain and another Ranger."

"Was it Clee Puttiphut?" asked my brother.

"No, it wasn't Clee. For a fact, as I recall, Clee was jest a mite too young yet. Him and me was good friends, but we hadn't truly hooked up as pardners with each other yet. This other Ranger was named Jameson, Charlie Jameson. If ever there was a man that Mother Nature had slobbered over, it was Charlie Jameson."

I looked at Tuck and he at me, but it was Mom who asked, "Was he very homely then?"

Great-uncle Hoyt chuckled but said nothing. He let Rudd reply.

"To the contrary, Floy. That ain't what I meant at all. That Charlie Jameson was so good-lookin' even cows turned their heads to gaze when he rode past. Though he had waving, coal-black hair, he was fair complected, with cheeks pink as a rose petal, teeth like pearls, and eyes blue as bluebonnet flowers. His nose was memorable for its straightness. He was gentle-spoken as a dove, and because of all them qualities everybody who met up with him soon came to dote on him." Great-uncle Rudd took a swallow of lemonade, made a face, and set the glass down on the veranda floor. "But after ridin' some time with Charlie, I got a different picture of him. He had took in the Texas Rangers, men that ain't usually fooled, by his meek and mild ways. He had a lot of papers, too, that testified to his fine character, letters sayin' what a good young snort he was. Naturally, I didn't read them papers, but

I heard plenty about 'em from everyone who read 'em. They claimed that he was a reg'lar churchgoer from somewheres in Missouri and that he come from a long line of preachers there and that he'd never been in a speck of trouble in all his twenty-five years of life. That last shoulda made me suspicious to start with."

"What was he truly like?" Mom wanted to know.

"Well, Floy, Kid Quiney—that's what they called me then—learned before long that Charlie Jameson was a fourth-rate cowboy but a first-rate killer. He wasn't no hand at all with cows. He couldn't use a rope worth a dang. He could ride a horse good like everybody else in the Texas Rangers, but whatever he'd done in his younger days, he hadn't never worked as a cowboy. As for his shootin', he was a dead shot all right. He seemed to take pleasure in shootin'. It appeared to me that Charlie Jameson shot everything that appeared in the countryside. He shot coyotes, prairie hens, buffalo, panthers, antelope, rattlesnakes, javelinas, any bird that could fly over or perched along the way, scorpions, and horned toads. He was a shootin' fool. Sometimes I'd catch him drawin' a bead on me or Captain as I rode along beside him—his idea of funnin'. I didn't find that entertainin' one bit and let him know, but he'd only laugh. After a time it seemed to me that he had a mean, cruel streak in his nature, and it made me wary. But I didn't know the half of it yet when it come to that man."

"Go on, please," Mom said, when he'd stopped to fumble in his pocket for his tobacco plug.

I gave my mother a look she should have understood because it was a glare, but she only smiled at me and put her finger to her lips.

Great-uncle Rudd got his tobacco into his jaw and said, "Well, sir, one night I woke up sudden at midnight to the howlin' of coyotes to find old Charlie gone and his horse and all his gear. What was worse—everything of mine was gone too, except for the bedroll I was snuggled down inside and my horse. The silver-mounted bridle and silver-mounted saddle I'd earned drivin' cows up to Kansas was gone. And so was my water canteen, all of my grub, and the saddle blanket. The only reason I still had Captain was that he was so much of a one-man horse that anybody who put his hand on him woulda been savaged to death at once. Charlie Jameson knowed that, so he hadn't gone near Captain. He also knowed I slept with my Colt revolver next to me in my blankets. No, siree, Jameson had snuck off with what he could get away with without no danger to his handsome hide. I supposed he'd been wantin' my silver horse gear for a long time, but bein' the wicked sneak he was, he never let me know about it. He was afraid of my scratching up his wishbone for him, and I woulda done it too!"

"What did you do now without any water?" asked Mom.

"To begin with, Floy, I told myself that I wasn't licked by a long shot yet. A Texas Ranger was supposed to ride like a Mexican, trail the enemy like a Indian, shoot like a Tennessean, and fight like a devil."

I couldn't help asking him, "Not like a fiend?"

"Nope, Mo, like a devil. There was a difference. When a man fights like a devil, he thinks while he's fightin'. Fiendish fightin' don't call for thought. Well, I figured Charlie knowed where he was bound if he lit out in the middle of the dark night. What he didn't know was that my time spent with Osage Indians had taught me how to track a man even if he was wadin' down the middle of a creek. So next mornin', with Captain followin' me, I started out walkin', lookin' for a sign of Jameson. Before long I found it, and we began followin' it, Captain and me. It led to a range of small hills with a gap between 'em. Drawin' my revolver, I started through it, fearin' to be ambushed in there. But I'd heard tell of the place sometime before, and I knowed there was a spring of water in there. Captain was in bad need of water, and I coulda used a drop or two myself by that time."

"And you were ambushed, weren't you?" Mom asked, fanning herself with the palm leaf.

"I surely was. Men with revolvers and rifles sprung up from behind big rocks on both sides. Among 'em was Charlie Jameson. His first words to me was, 'So you tracked me down, Kid Quiney? Now you have been caught good an' proper. Throw down your Colt. These here are my kinfolks, Jesse and Frank,' and he rattled off about six more names."

"The James brothers! Oh, boy!" Tuck clutched Brownie so hard she yipped, wriggled loose, jumped down, and ran off the porch down into the rose garden.

"Yes, sir, you bet. Old Charlie's real name was James, not Jameson at all. In case you was wonderin' why a James boy outlaw would join up with the Texas Rangers, it was because that way one of that evil gang would know all the Rangers' secrets and tricks and be able to fight fire with fire.

"Now Charlie said to the others, 'This here's the Quiney Kid. He is noted for his red hair and his quick temper. Be careful of him.'

"I didn't say anything to Charlie at all. Instead, as I let my Colt fall out of my hand, I said, 'Will somebody water my horse, please?'

" 'I'll do that,' came a ringing voice. Out from behind the man called Jesse darted a slip of a gal with raven-black locks over her shoulders. She come trippin' forward, picked up my revolver, and stuck it into her belt, all the time starin' up into my eyes. Except for bein' a gal, she was the spittin' image of Charlie—even to blue eyes. She turned out to be his little sister, Zuleika, and jest sixteen years old."

"*Zuleika*!" exclaimed Tuck. "Where did you get that name?"

"Purty, ain't it? Well, she was purtier than her name, and she was the princess of them fierce outlaws. While she was lookin' me over, the scowlin' outlaw by the name of Frank asked, 'Shall we pecos this little Ranger and have done with him right away?'

"Hearin' that made my blood freeze up in my veins, though I didn't let on. I was in trouble like a mule up a bush. I knowed what it meant to be pecosed. It meant bein' shot dead, ripped open, stuffed full of rocks, and dumped in a river, never to be found again.

"The gal looked away from me now and called out to them outlaws, 'There ain't any river anywheres near here, only that little crick with hardly no water in it.' By Gatlin's, that gal was on my side! She'd saved me. She yelled out now, 'Charlie, dear, I seen that handsome silver saddle and bridle of his you brought in. Has this Ranger got any family that you know about?'

"Colt in hand, Charlie come up to me too. He nodded at her. 'He surely does, Zuleika, honey. There's more Quineys down in Santa Rosa County than you could shake a stick at.'

" 'Are they rich, Charlie?'

" 'I dunno, Zuleika. He said that they own a horse and mule ranch. Some of them are still livin' on it. His oldest brother runs the spread.'

" 'What's his name?' the outlaw gal asked me, holding my own revolver on me.

" 'Earl Beauregard Quiney.'

" 'Would he pay a ransom to save your life?' she wanted to know next.

"This gave me hope, hope of escapin' in time, so I said, 'He's my own flesh-and-blood brother, ain't he?'

" 'All right,' were her words. 'Gimme that ruby ring you got on your finger, and it'll travel to your brother as a sign that we got you. There'll be a letter goin' along with it. After somebody starts on his way with it, I'll water your horse.'

"It seemed to me now that her eyes were a cold-blooded blue. I hated partin' with that ruby-stone ring I'd won in a game of chance, but there wasn't no help for it. Surely Earl would know it inasmuch as I'd won it off him by drawin' kings whereas he drew queens. I pulled it off and gave it to her, and then when she'd pocketed it and started toward Captain, I said to her, 'Ma'am, if you know what's good for you, you won't touch that horse of mine. He don't like it.'

" 'That's right, Zuleika, honey,' came from her brother. 'Otherwise I would have nabbed him too and been rid of this Quiney Kid forevermore.'

"I said, 'No, you wouldn't, Charlie Jameson. I didn't mount him once on the way here trackin' you. I walked to spare my horse.'

"This made the little old gal eye me with respect. She knew that all cowboys surely hate to walk. She said, 'Thank you, Kid, for warnin' me about your horse. I surely hope your brother will pay $500 for you. I say this is what we ought to ask for.'

"That knocked me back on my hocks. That was a lot of cash, and I couldn't say that I'd parted with Earl on the best of terms when I rode off to join the Texas Rangers. I almost never did part on good terms with him.

"Well, sir, things moved fast for a little while after that. I watered Captain and myself down by the crick while them outlaws sent a rider south to Santa Rosa County with a letter Zuleika wrote to Earl and with my ruby ring.

"But after he'd rode off, things moved slow as a

sore-footed jackass. There was some shacks and a corral built inside that outlaw stronghold down by the crick. I was kept handcuffed, which was a humiliation to me, because they was my own Texas Ranger handcuffs. Other than that, I wasn't treated too bad. Charlie and Frank and Jesse was in and out of the stronghold, robbin' and killin'. The folks that stayed there all the time was Zuleika and an old man who done the cookin' for the gang. The gal used to come talk to me and ask about the Quineys when she wasn't playin' the guitar. She was a good guitar player and enlivened the days and nights while we all waited for Earl to reply.

"Finally that rider they sent out come back. Charlie was there in the stronghold when he did. Him and me and Jesse listened to the message as Zuleika read out loud. It was short. Earl had got somebody to read it for him and write an answer. It said, 'Rudd got himself into this mess. He can get himself out of it. Tell him thanks for the return of the ring. I found out later on how he'd cheated in that poker game.'

"After readin' this, Zuleika looked at me mournfully and said, 'Your brother ain't got much family feelin', has he?'

" 'No, ma'am, he don't seem to.' I was starin' at Charlie, not at her. He had his hand too near his Colt to comfort me.

"She saw where his hand was too, and she said, 'Charlie, maybe Kid Quiney's brother didn't understand the message we sent. Let's try it one more time. Let's send off somethin' else that belongs to the Kid.'

" 'All right, Zuleika,' said Jesse. 'This time let's send him somethin' that he can't say was his to begin with. Not the Kid's revolver or his boots, something personal!'

"Oh, how that outlaw was starin' at me. His gaze was both mean and memorable!

" 'Jesse, we could send him one of the Kid's fingers,' said Charlie. 'I noticed once that the Kid's got a crooked little finger on his right hand.'

"Now that was so. A mule had stepped on it and mashed it when I'd been a weaner and crawled into the mule pen on our ranch. It had never been much use to me ever since. Earl oughta remember that finger all right. But I didn't cotton to the idea of bein' nine-fingered very much.

" 'Ain't there any other parts of the Kid that his brother might know by sight?' asked Zuleika, who of all them outlaws was most on my side. 'What do you say, Kid?'

"Being' asked such a thing truly set me to thinkin' hard. Not that my finger was so handsome, but I was surely attached to it—or rather it was attached to me. I mean, I could wiggle it. But then I could wiggle most of my parts. Then I bethought myself of my hair, so I said, 'How about sendin' Earl some cuttings of my hair?'

"This made Charlie and Jesse and the gal ponder. Then Charlie shook his head. 'No, that won't do. Kid Quiney ain't the only one in the country with carrot-colored locks. For that matter, there's many a cow that leans to his shade of red, and not a few horses I have seen. What's to stop his brother from convincin' himself we roached a horse's mane or currycombed a old stray steer?'

"Curse the luck, Charlie was right. Folks had commented that my head was a mite cow-colored. Tuggin' on my right earlobe the way I always did when I was thinkin' deeply, I come up with another idea. I told 'em, 'The bottom part of my left ear has three little bitty moles on it. Earl would recall them, I bet.'

" 'He might at that.' Zuleika came directly up to me, stood on her tiptoes, lifted my hair, and peeked at my left ear. 'Yes, siree,' she said, 'the moles are jest where he said they was. The ear ought to do jest fine.'

"So that's what went down to Santa Rosa County the next mornin', wrapped up in a handkerchief of Zuleika's, with a letter wrapped around the handkerchief. It was Zuleika herself who cut off the part as tenderly as she could with some sewin' shears. It was that little gal who held my hand and soothed my pain with whiskey and put cobwebs on the ear to stop the bleedin' afterwards.

"And so we waited some more and finally back rode the bandit's messenger again. I had a sinkin' feelin' in my gizzard as he dismounted, because he was not smilin' in greetin' to his fellow outlaws. I figgered that Earl had failed me again, and so he had. Once more I listened to what the messenger gave to Zuleika to read to me, Charlie, Jesse, and this time to old Frank James, too. The message said that Earl had looked at the ear part and believed it might belong to me, but he could only truly recall two moles as bein' on my earlobe, so he wasn't sure about the ear bein' mine. He also said that he didn't have $500 to ransom me, but he was willin' to ride up to their robbers' roost, if the bandits would tell him where it was, and escort me home without his askin' them for a nickel for the pleasure of my charmin' company all this time.'

"That sent them outlaws into a fit of spite, let me tell you. They took a vote and decided then and there that they were goin' to shoot me in the mornin', because they was all pullin' out of their stronghold for someplace west in New Mexico Territory. By now I knowed too much about them to go on livin'. They were gonna shoot Captain too, because no man could manage my faithful mount but me.

"Because they knowed I was desperate now that I'd heard my death sentence, they took off the handcuffs I'd been wearin' and bound me hand and foot with rawhide and then left me on a bunk down in the cabin closest to the crick. While I lay reflectin' on all the bad things I'd done that might keep me out of Heaven and all the good things I shoulda done to get me past them Pearly Gates, the locked cabin door was opened very softly. It was little old Zuleika come to say farewell and try to get a willin' kiss from my lips. She'd been after a kiss ever since I got captured, but I'd refused to give her one willingly. Because she was sobbin' and carryin' on now, and because I was tied hand and foot instead of jest handcuffed, I let her kiss me, but all the same I still didn't kiss her back. I'd made it a motto never to kiss outlaws."

"Oh, my gosh!" said Tuck.

"That's right. That was one of my mottoes then, Tuck. I heard the gal say something' after she kissed me that made me prick up my ears, though. She said, 'Kid Quiney, if I leave the cabin door open, you might be able to make it down to the crick to say farewell to Captain, too.' And out she went weepin' quietly.

"Naturally, I wanted to see my horse again, so I rolled myself off that bunk and over the cabin floor to the open door. I wiggled myself through that and out onto the little porch. Rolling across it too, I landed on the ground below. Now it was danged hard goin' over dirt and sharp rocks to that crick. Once I rolled next to a cactus and got stuck. The only good thing I could see about it was that it was downhill all the way to the crick, and because the night was wet and stormy nobody on guard heard me or saw me rollin' along.

"Finally I made it to the edge of the crick, but I found that I had picked up too much downhill speed. I rolled right off the bank into the water, which was icy cold. There wasn't no way of gettin' out of the crick bottom either, because I surely couldn't roll myself up the other side. I resigned myself to drownin', instead of bein' shot. But there was a nearby rock not far from where I landed, and I half swam like a fish over to it and put my chin up on it so I could breathe. And there I lay most of the rest of that night with water runnin' over me and rain pourin' down on me, sometimes cussin' Earl but mostly prayin'."

"My!" exclaimed Mom, drinking the last of her

lemonade. "Uncle Rudd, what helped you most—the cursing or the praying?"

"The prayin', Floy. Prayin' has powers. You know, that water loosened up the rawhide straps so much that before long they floated clear off my wrists and ankles. I was free! I rose up out of the crick froze to the bones but still able to crawl to the bandits' corral. I reached up silent as a serpent and let down the bar that kept the outlaws' horses in. Then I called out Captain's name, which he knew well. He come out to me right away as I knowed that good animal would. I pulled myself up beside him by holdin' on first to his tail; then I grabbed hold of his mane and swung aboard him. Quiet as could be, guidin' him by my knees and whispers, him and me went around the corral, nudgin' them other horses out of it. Knowin' the nature of horses, I got out in front of the bunch. Then I set Captain to a trot, and sure as could be all them other horses followed his lead away, like ghosts in the rainy, thunderin' night. Because they were so sure of their hideout bein' a secret, the outlaws had set only one guard that night and he didn't see Captain and me and all them horses gettin' clear away. More than that, the guard was drunk, because the gang was celebratin' their leavin' the night before they left.

"Well, sir, they didn't celebrate the next mornin', when they got up with big headaches from drinkin' so much and found there wasn't nothing to ride away on.

"As for me, I made my way to a town where I found another Texas Ranger and made my report to him. Some more Rangers rode back up there and captured them outlaws—all but Jesse and Frank, who'd gone elsewhere. Charlie and Zuleika turned out to be second cousins once removed of the James brothers. Them two went to prison. Charlie got hung by the neck until dead, but little Zuleika served her sentence and finally got set free to lead a better life. At heart she wasn't all bad. I rejoiced to hear that she turned out all right in the end."

Then Great-uncle Rudd gave Mom a grin and asked, "Floy, what do you think of my life as a Texas Ranger?"

"Oh, I think it must have been splendid to be a real one, Uncle Rudd."

"It was, Floy." He turned to me. "What do you think, Mo?"

I said, "I think it was almost as good a story as the one about Avarilla Arrowwood, but I don't believe it either."

"Why don'tcha?"

"Because you said that you never learned to read. And if that was so, and that's one thing I do believe, you couldn't read a list of criminals the Texas Rangers gave you."

"You got yourself a point there, Mo. I'll grant you that." He took off his hat, fanned his face with it, and laughed. Then he said, "Powerful hot, ain't it?"

"It'll rain before mornin'," Great-uncle Hoyt said. "Even if there ain't a cloud in the sky right at this minute, it'll rain."

"Is that a gospel truth?" I asked him while I looked at Rudd.

"It's gospel, Mo," answered Great-uncle Hoyt.

9
The Big Blow

I was annoyed that I seemed to be the only one of my family who was as impatient with Great-uncle Rudd's terrible lying as we all ought to have been. Tuck egged him on, just as if the tales he told were the exciting fairy stories Mom used to read aloud to us when we were little. Even if she refused to listen to his awful lies, Grandmother was determined to forgive him, and even if she wouldn't tell us what he'd done out in San Diego, it seemed to me that she was forgiving him too much here in MacRae. And my own mother was becoming as bad as my brother! I never would have expected Mom to sit through one of his horrible long whoppers all the way—much less approve of it. I surely didn't understand her.

I didn't understand Great-uncle Hoyt either or Mrs. Hemmrich. They were more patient with Great-uncle Rudd than I was. Was I ever glad that we'd be leaving Wednesday morning! I was counting the hours.

When Mom came in off the veranda later that day, she found me sitting alone in the stuffy parlor waiting for her. I'd hoped she'd come in without my brother or either of the Quiney men. "Mom," I said, "can I talk with you for a minute?"

"Yes, Merle, you *may*." She corrected my grammar, which showed me that at least she wasn't beginning to talk like my great-uncles. "But don't take too long. I want to go out to the kitchen and get my wrist in some hot water now."

"All right, Mom." I came straight to the point. "You really liked that awful story about the bandits, and you sort of liked the one about the blizzard. You laughed in the places he wanted you to laugh. How could you do it?"

Her head tilted to one side as she looked at the bandage on her wrist. "Yes, I did laugh, and I listened. It made him happy, or didn't you notice that?"

"I sure did notice it. That's what I'm talking about."

"Merle, your Great-uncle Rudd doesn't have much of a life here, you know. According to Mrs. Hemmrich, he never was a success. He never became rich or important or famous for anything. Many men find being successful the most important thing there is. He never had that pleasure. He's very old-fashioned, you know."

"Uh-huh. He doesn't like short skirts and short hair. He doesn't like it to be 1929, does he?"

"No, I doubt if he does. Mrs. Hemmrich and your Great-uncle Hoyt are fairly content to live here where they seldom see anyone but each other. They have that sort of personality. They're gentle souls at heart. But your Great-uncle Rudd is different. He would like a bigger world than MacRae, so he continually makes up worlds he claims he was very important in. He has adventures in them because he can't have adventures in everyday life and never really did have. Did you know that he hasn't a penny of his own? He lives off the charity of his brother Hoyt."

I shook my head. "No, nobody told me that, Mom." I had a thought. "Do you suppose that's why he tells those stories—to entertain Hoyt because they don't have a radio?"

"No, dear, unless they amuse Hoyt because he likes to see how people react to his brother. He must have heard them a hundred times over the years." Mom bent over and put her good hand on my arm. "I think Rudd tells them to keep himself from being unhappy because he's poor and old and things aren't ever going to be any better for him than they are right now. And he has another reason for being downhearted, you know."

"What's that? His arthritis? It seems to me he makes the medicine he wants for that."

"Merle, his time is over in more ways than one. He's too old to do the kind of work he once did, but what's even worse the world he lived in is gone now. There aren't any real Wild West bandits anymore. There really isn't any Old West anymore."

I said, "In the picture shows there is." But I knew that they were make-believe. "Grandmother brags to Mrs. Hemmrich about how modern and up-to-date you are. But you like to hear about the 1870's and 1880's. How come, Mom?"

"A person who is modern can still appreciate what's past. A modern person can pick and choose what was best about the past, can't she?"

I snorted. "Yes, Billy bedamned, long gone by. I'm tired of hearing him say that and start another big lie."

"Merle, it's all he has that gives him pleasure, and, remember, he's sharing that pleasure with others, his listeners."

I said, "It isn't fair that he gets away with it. You wouldn't let Graham or me tell whoppers like Rudd does. You'd take away our allowances or tell us no more picture shows, and Dad might take a switch to us."

"No, we wouldn't like you to lie, but you and your brother have your lives ahead of you. We hope that you both will have better lives than Rudd did."

I asked, "Are you going to send Dad one of those postcards saying that we were visiting in MacRae and had a wonderful time?"

"Yes, I am. The minute I get to a place that has postcards. And this time I'm really going to mean what I write on the card. I am having a fine time here. But at this moment I have to go soak my wrist."

She went out, leaving me as cross as ever. Old Rudd Quiney was a dreadful liar, and he was getting away with it, and even being admired for it. Well, I couldn't do anything about his lies, but maybe I could get in a few licks at him somehow. So I went out onto the veranda, crossed it, and walked down into the front garden to get Brownie, who was sniffing rosebushes.

Holding the squirming dog in my arms, I marched right up to Great-uncle Rudd and said, "I'm tired of having Grandmother's dog walking all over me all night out in the car—particularly when it's hot. The dog's hot too. There's plenty of room in your guest room for a dog as little as this. How about being nicer to our dog?"

"What do you think, Rudd?" Great-uncle Hoyt looked at his brother.

Rudd leaned forward in his horn chair, opened his mouth, and spat a stream of tobacco juice all the way over the veranda railing onto the ground near some marigolds. "I done that jest right, Hoyt. Didn't hit a single flower." Then he peered at Brownie. "It's all right with me, though I never have held much with earwig-size dogs since that time in Missouri when I lost part of my ear and my old dog Slacker was bad affected too."

Ye Gods! Another story! I told him what I figured Mom would like. "Great-uncle Rudd, please don't tell it till tomorrow sometime. Our mom will want to hear it too. She's out soaking her wrist and will be doing that until bedtime."

"Sure, Mo, I'll hold the story. I've told Tuck two already today."

"No, it's three stories—the bullwhips, the blizzard, and the outlaws," said my brother.

"That's enough stories for anybody," said the old man. "Tuck ought to be jest about tuckered out from all that listenin'." Great-uncle Hoyt laughed along with Rudd, but my brother and I didn't. Being named Tucker, we'd heard that joke too often.

Then Graham said, "I've never heard you mention Slacker in any other story before, but you talked about his being so fast he could outrun a horse."

"True, true—he could for very short distances. Tomorrow you'll hear more about that remarkable animal. Mo, you go tell your grandma she can have that dog in her bed with her tonight if she wants to."

"Thank you." I spoke to Great-uncle Hoyt, not to Rudd. Then I went into the house and out to the kitchen, where I put Brownie down at Grandmother's feet with the words, "She can sleep in your room from now on. I asked the uncles for you, and they said okay."

"Why thank you, Merle." Grandmother was peeling apples and smiling at me. Mom and Mrs. Hemmrich were smiling too as Brownie walked over to her bowl of leftover roast chicken.

I went on. "Great-uncle Rudd seems to think Brownie isn't as good as his dog, Slacker."

"Slacker?" Grandmother put down the knife she was using into the bowl with the apples. Her eyes seemed to be staring away into the distance behind her glasses. "I hadn't thought of Slacker in fifty years until Rudd mentioned him the other day."

"Then he was a real dog, Grandmother?"

"Oh, yes, he was. He was Rudd's dog. Down on the ranch we always had dogs. I can only remember the names of two of them, J.E.B. Stuart and Slacker."

I asked next, "Was Captain a real horse then?"

"I don't know, Merle. I never set eyes on him."

"Captain was a real horse. I saw him," said Mrs. Hemmrich. "He lived long enough to be the oldest horse in the state, according to Rudd and Hoyt."

I turned to Mom, who was sitting at the table with

her wrist in hot water. "Great-uncle Rudd promised me that he won't tell the story of how he lost part of his ear in Missouri until tomorrow, so you can be there to hear it too. He says Slacker's in that story."

"Missouri?" Mrs. Hemmrich was doing some fancy-work on a piece of cloth held in an oval embroidery hoop. She shook her head. "I'd thought by now that I'd heard them all, but I don't remember any ear story that takes place in Missouri—or one that has a dog in it. I guess I might as well listen to that one too. I suppose I should keep up with Rudd's tales."

Mom said, "Maybe it's true." She laughed and added, "You know there has to be a true story somewhere. The lobe of his left ear really is missing."

Grandmother was busy with the paring knife again. "That story might be forgotten by now. Doesn't Hoyt know the truth, Carolina?"

"Susannah, I asked Hoyt several times years ago when I first came here. He would never give me an answer. All Hoyt would ever do was grin at me."

"He must have learned that trick from Rudd." Grandmother sighed as she finished the last pie apple. "You know, Carolina, I do believe Hoyt was right when he said it would rain. The air's growing thicker all the time."

I said, as I stood on tiptoe to look out between Mrs. Hemmrich's blue-and-white checked kitchen curtains, "The sky is getting grayer."

All at once and for no reason at all, Grandmother said, "Floy, our Merle's shooting up these days like a plant. She's quite a girl too. Only the best of the Quiney blood's seemed to come down to her. I like the way she stands up to Rudd, that old longhorn, and I liked the way she asked a favor for Brownie and me, and I particularly like what she told you out in the parlor a while back about objecting to his lies."

My jaw must have fallen a full foot, I was so astonished. A *compliment* from Grandmother, said right out where I could hear it!

I was speechless, but not Mom. She said, "Why thank you, Mother. Yes, I think Merle is a child to be proud of, and so is Graham."

Mrs. Hemmrich had the last word. "As you say, Floy, they were both born under earth signs, one a Virgo, the other a Taurus. That will give them level heads if nothing else will. Your mother is a Capricorn, another earth sign."

And now they started off on what sign Mom was and why she was so modern, and I just sat and listened while I watched the sky through the curtains get darker and darker until we had to turn on the kitchen lights.

Oh, how it rained during the night! And it got lots colder. I wished now that I had Brownie to keep me warm. It seemed to me that I lay on the back seat of the Studebaker awake with my head under the covers half the night, hoping that the shut windows wouldn't leak and I wouldn't get dripped on.

In the morning the road was a mess of red-colored mud. The ruts were full of brown-red water. Though it had quit raining, the sky was still cloudy gray in most places. Graham and I went into the house together, but before we got inside Grandmother met us on the porch and opened the screen door to let Brownie out.

She said, "Hurry up and get dressed. Breakfast's almost ready. Rudd and Hoyt are starting in on their flannel cakes."

"Heck," Graham grumbled, as we went down the hall to the bathroom. "We're too late to see if old Rudd licks the syrup jug. I've been waiting for us to have hot cakes so I could find out."

"Cheer up, Tuck," I told him. "You've seen Great-uncle Hoyt with his thumb in the coffee a couple of times." I poked him in the ribs. "Hey, it's Monday. We've only got one more day here. Aren't you going to miss watching Hoyt drink his coffee that way when we've gone?"

"No, but I think I'll miss some other things around here—like the horse and the stories." He stopped at the door of the bathroom and said, "Sometimes Great-uncle Rudd's like somebody out of a motion picture. Sort of like the cowboy William S. Hart, except that William S. Hart isn't really funny."

I thought for a minute, then nodded, thinking of what Mom had said to me yesterday in the parlor. But William S. Hart would never lie.

This Monday morning Mrs. Hemmrich and Grandmother stayed seated at the breakfast table after they'd stacked the dirty dishes on the top of the sideboard. I was sent to the kitchen for the coffeepot, and after I'd come back and filled everybody's cup to the top again, Mom said, "Uncle Rudd, we're all waiting to hear about your life in Missouri."

"Thank you kindly, Floy. You too, Carolina, and you, Susie, gal?"

"Yes, Rudd, we are," said Mrs. Hemmrich. "I don't recall hearing anything ever about Missouri or a dog you had."

"I don't believe that you have." With one of Hoyt's cigars waggling in his teeth, he came out with the words I'd been expecting. "Billy bedamned, it was long gone by, but I remember the year of 1878 in Missouri as clear as if it was last week. Me and Clee Puttiphut and little Ruby Nell, we went from Santa Rosa County to try our hands at wheat farmin'. I was weary of Texas by then. I'd been let out of the Texas Rangers sometime before because of some cruel wounds I took in a gunfight down near the Mexican border. Since that time I'd tried to raise mules with Earl on the ranch, but I seemed to grow so many blisters on his temper, I'd quit that and rode north with Clee to do cowboy work for that Englishman, that Mr. Morehouse, and look after them loco Red Dundalks of his. And you know how bad that work went, because I told you all about it."

"I hear you told the children about my bad knitting," Grandmother said very quietly. "Rudd, in all my born days I never knit one stitch for you."

Hoyt put in, "Susie, I heard you say once a long time ago that if you ever took up knittin', you'd be tempted to knit Rudd a chokestrap necktie."

"A noose is what I had in mind then." Grandmother shifted in her chair, sighed, and said, "Go on, Rudd. Amuse us."

"I surely will try to do that, Susie. Well, sir, me and Clee took one of the Puttiphut wagons, and with Ruby Nell, who planned on keepin' house for her brother and me, we started on our way to Missouri. I was naturally ridin' Captain, and Clee was ridin' Harley. Ruby Nell was a good hand with mules, so she drove the wagon. There wasn't no animal brute, cow or horse or even mule, that didn't cotton at once to that little old gal. She had to be the purtiest little thing a sore-eyed man ever set eyes on. My redbone hound, Slacker, doted on her, she was so sweet-natured. Slacker, he come along with us to Missouri, runnin' all the way alongside Captain and Harley, when he wasn't restin' in the wagon."

"Yes, Ruby Nell was sweet-natured," agreed Mrs. Hemmrich, nodding.

"What did she look like?" Mom wanted to know. "Was she prettier than the outlaw girl, Zuleika?" She was smiling.

"Ruby Nell surely was. That's one of the reasons I didn't take up with that bandit princess, Floy, because my heart was always set on Ruby Nell from the time we was little more than weaners. After Ruby Nell died, it took me four years before I could speak her name. You want to know what she looked like. She wasn't no higher'n my heart, she was so small. She had the softest hair you ever saw. It was pale yellow color, almost the color of a buckskin horse or taffy candy. Her eyes was so deep a brown you could never see to the bottom of 'em. She didn't have more'n six freckles across her nose all the years I knowed her. I liked 'em, though she didn't. Buttermilk and lemon juice mixed together never would take 'em away, though she kept tryin' year after year to get rid of them freckles. She sang like a bird, and she always smelled of rose water. Everybody doted on her—even Hoyt here. He woulda married her if she woulda asked him, wouldn't you, Hoyt?"

"Yes, sir, Rudd, she was our county's yellow rose of Texas."

Rudd went on. "Me and Clee and Ruby Nell found us a farm where we could raise wheat. We was rentin' it, plannin' to pay back the man who owned it with part of what we made out of our first crop. It was a nice spread, with a house to live in, a strong-made log barn, a pigsty, and some other farm buildins'. What we didn't know about it when we moved in was why the Missouri farmer who rented it to us had moved out. We Texans learned why danged fast, though. It was because of our neighbor, that devil of a galoot on the farm to the south of us, old man Bremer."

"What did he do?" asked Mom.

"First of all, he made it clear he didn't favor folks from Texas. He said in the nearby town that me and Clee wasn't only one-time Texas cattle rustlers, but we'd been around cows so long we was growin' horns and had hair all over us and that we ate grass in preference to bacon and eggs. He claimed that Ruby Nell dyed her hair yellow and that my dog Slacker was the worst egg-suckin' dog in all of Texas and a chicken killer to boot."

"Why did he hate you so much?" asked Mrs. Hemmrich, almost as if she believed his story.

"Because he was a damnyankee. And me and Clee didn't make no secret in Missouri of the fact that we sided by the Confederacy, and if we'd been old enough to be soldiers, we woulda fought like fiends for the cause of the South. The man who rented us the farm was a Confederate too. That man and old Bremer had had a lot of trouble with that barbed wire Bremer put up. Me and Clee, we soon learned about Bremer's barbed wire too. Like every other cattleman, we Texans hated barbed wire. With barbed wire a man could enclose a crick or river, so thirsty cows couldn't get to the water or to shelter in a storm. Bremer strung barbed wire to close off the road to town when he took a notion to, so me or Clee would have to cut his wire to pass. He did that to rile us Texans and drive us off the farm. But the worst things about our bad neighbor were his hog and his wife."

"His wife and his hog?" exclaimed Mom.

"Yep, Floy. His wife was a poor, little old woman who looked to us like she never seen a well day in her life, and he never gave a kind word to her or his three kids. He was fonder by far of that hog he called Jim Chester, because it was a Chester White hog. Jim Chester was a prizewinner at the county fair every year. Mrs. Bremer would never win any prizes anywhere. We was sorry for her. Now, sir, that hog was near as big as a cow, near five feet high at the shoulder. He had a mean disposition and meant murder. Captain and Harley purely hated the sight of Jim Chester. Horses don't favor the company of hogs till they get to know 'em real good, and with Jim Chester that never could be. I can still hear Captain snortin' to this day, when he spotted Jim Chester standin' behind Bremer's barbed-wire fence glarin' at us. Captain and Harley would both put back their ears and lash their tails when they knew that big pig was nearby. As for Slacker, the hound went plumb crazy when he got the hog's scent. Ruby Nell was scared out of her wits by the brute, where nothin' else that had hide, horns, feathers, or fur had ever bothered her.

"That Jim Chester had his little ways, let me tell you. He was a smart hog. He'd learned how to dig his way out of his sty on Bremer's place and come over the fields to our place and wiggle under the barbed wire into our farmyard. Many's the time me and Clee would come out in the mornin' ready to do some plowin' on the south forty and find Jim Chester sittin' on his back haunches out in front of the veranda, snufflin' at us, starin' cruelly at us out of them red pig eyes of his.

"It got so he'd come sneakin' over in the middle of the night. I'd know when Jim Chester had arrived, because Slacker would ease out from under my head where he was doin' his duty as my pillow. Then he'd howl his head off because he was so upset by that hog. You see, Slacker didn't have no fun at all in Missouri. Back home in Texas on our ranch, he used to drive folks up a fence post. Then he'd walk around the post pretendin' to be fierce and feisty. We called what he was doin' 'treein' trespassers.'

"Here in Missouri we was all bein' treed by Jim Chester! He had it in mind to chew us to shreds, that hog did. That animal had a hide like a underdone beef-steak, and so did old man Bremer, come to think of it. Him and his Jim Chester looked enough alike to be father and son."

Mom giggled. I didn't laugh at what he'd said, though. I was watching Mrs. Hemmrich. She seemed to be listening carefully. *Maybe this story was true*!

"What did you Texans do about Jim Chester?" asked my brother.

"We kept out of the hog's way. Me and Clee considered shootin' him and dinin' on ham and pork chops for a season, but he was a valuable hog, and the whole county knew him by name and sight. Because of his size and mean disposition, folks seemed sort of proud of him. Too, they didn't have to live next door to him. It was the sheriff of the county who told me and Clee that Jim Chester was a hunderd-dollar hog and whoever made bacon out of him was goin' to have to pay that much money to old man Bremer and more'n likely a twenty-dollar fine to boot for the crime of shootin' the brute. Me and Clee wasn't flush with cash. We was close to broke.

"Finally, me and Clee and Ruby Nell made up our minds that we'd have to leave Missouri for somewhere's else before everybody's nerves cracked because of the

Bremer pig. Slacker was so bad off by now he spent all his time under my bed at night instead of bein' on top of it where he belonged, bein' my pillow. We was goin' to tell the farmer who owned the place as we went through the town he was livin' in that we was goin' away for good. This was so he could send somebody brave out to look after his milk cows and his chickens.

"Little Ruby Nell was sadly packin' her trunks, gettin' ready to leave the county, when old Mother Nature took a hand in matters. What happened was the last thing in the world we expected, let me tell you."

"Another blizzard?" asked Mom.

"No, Floy, it wasn't. It was July and hotter'n the hinges of hell. I hadn't knowed till then that Missouri could be so hot as Texas. It was so danged hot that mornin' we planned to head for Texas, we stayed on for fear of Ruby Nell's wagon mules gettin' sunstroke and dyin' in their traces. The only good thing about the heat was that it made Jim Chester stay home to wallow in the mud of his sty. Hogs sunburn, in case you didn't know it."

"We didn't," said Mom.

"It's gospel truth," volunteered Great-uncle Hoyt.

"Hoyt's right. Well, so me and Clee and Ruby Nell sat out on the veranda gaspin' for breath, jest waitin' for the heat spell to snap. It didn't show any inclination to until the afternoon of the fourth day. That's when the sky clouded over so as to make a person think rain was on the way. We was hopin' for it to cool things off. After a while it got quite a bit colder, and then the thunder started rollin' overhead. It thundered worse than I'd ever heard it thunder in Texas while we waited for the rain to begin. But the rain didn't come and it didn't come, which we all considered to be mighty peculiar.

"Ruby Nell had gone to the barn to comfort her mules and was on her way back to the veranda when we saw her stop still in the barnyard with her mouth open and her dainty hands pressed to her bosom. I thought she'd spied Jim Chester, but then decided that couldn't be it unless he was up on the roof this time. Her eyes was fixed higher than that even. They was set on the top of the big hill that stood behind the house. When I called out to ask the gal what was the matter, she didn't say one word. She only pointed with a tremblin' arm.

"Now I came down off the veranda with Clee, and we looked to the hill too. It was so dark a color it appeared to be covered with smoke from a fire. Was we about to be burned out? But what we was seein' wasn't fire, and it wasn't ground sweat or fog neither. It was a tornado.

"And then it hit—that tornado did! The second after I'd grabbed Ruby Nell up in my arms and carried her into the house, it struck us. For a wonder it caught all of us in the house where we'd be a mite safer than outside. Slacker, he was in the safest place of all—under my bed.

"From the house windows we looked out, and what did we see but sticks and logs flyin' about in all directions. The chicken coop soon went sailin' past, followed by a couple of speckled hens squawkin' and lookin' more like feather dusters than chickens. After that the barn split, and them big logs that used to be the barn flew by. Next came the corral railin's rattlin' against each other like drumsticks. We couldn't see for all the dust and dirt and other stuff in the air what had happened to Captain and Harley and the mules.

"With her arms around my neck, Ruby Nell let out cries I'll never forget as the tornado hit the house. It wasn't as if the big blow hit it head on. It sort of whirled around the house like it was checkin' it out to see how much it weighed. And after that tornado found out, it decided that the house wasn't too heavy to lift."

"What did it do?" Mom asked.

"It lifted up the house, Floy!"

I exploded, "Oh, my gosh!" I didn't believe a word of this.

"Merle, tornadoes have done some very queer things," said Mrs. Hemmrich.

"This Missouri one surely did, Carolina." Great-uncle Rudd went on. "Well, as I said, it wrenched that farmhouse right up off the root cellar and sent it whirlin' and swirlin' around and around in the sky. We was all on the floor by now, hangin' onto furniture that was skiddin' hither and thither and this way and that way as the house kept tiltin'. Finally the old tornado got the house where it wanted it, sailin' along in a straight line. It was steady enough now for me to crawl to the open window, pull myself up, hold tight to the sill, and look out over it. We must of been hunderds of feet up in the air, and judgin' from landmarks below us we was travelin' due south. But other things were travelin' due north, comin' straight toward us. It was a wide tornado. Either that, or it was two tornadoes going in opposite directions. We never did find out which. Them things travelin' north come straight at us. We could hear 'em hittin' the outside walls—shovels, hoes, rakes, horse collars, and all sorts of things. They was all comin' from the Bremer place. I could tell because Mrs. Bremer's red-and-white zigzag quilt, which I recognized from seein' it on her wash line, went by with all them other things.

"After them pitiful objects come the most amazing thing of all—old Bremer's house. It come along, passin' the one we was in like we was two sailin' ships on the sea, not houses at all. That old damnyankee devil Bremer was lookin' out his window too. When he spied me, he shook his fist at me and yelled out somethin' insultin', so I leaned out too and shook my fist at him.

"And then jest as his house went whiskin' past, along come his choppin' block with the axe in it. At that very moment the axe got loose from the block. Sharp as could be, it headed straight for me almost as if Bremer had aimed it—not the tornado. I turned my head fast as I could to save my nose from bein' cut off. Because of that swift and smart action my nose was saved, but the blade of the axe nicked me on the bottom of my left ear before I could draw in my head all the way. That tornado took part of me away with it forevermore."

Mom put her face into her hands, but I could see

her shoulders heaving as she laughed. Grandmother wasn't laughing. She was staring at a crack in the ceiling, and Mrs. Hemmrich was smiling and nodding. Great-uncle Hoyt was grinning at my brother, who was grinning too.

No one said a word, but that didn't stop Great-uncle Rudd, who wasn't finished yet. He said, "I thought the house we was flyin' along in would never settle down, but it did finally. It come to rest smack-dab on the exact spot where the Bremer house had been. There was some damage done, though. We landed gentle enough so none of us got hurt, but when we come to earth, our veranda busted off. It bounced over the barnyard into Bremer's pigsty, where Jim Chester was cowerin' in the mud to keep from bein' swept away too. One of the veranda posts hit the big old hog on the head and killed him stone dead."

Mom looked up, chuckling. "What did you do then?"

"We rejoiced, Floy. We rejoiced because we hadn't been killed and our pig enemy had. We all gave thanks, then turned to and butchered Jim Chester after Captain and Harley and the mules came to where we were by tracking us. We was all happy, even Slacker who couldn't see hisself in a mirror or he would not have been pleased at all."

"Why not, Uncle Rudd?"

"That fright he got from the tornado turned him from a red hound to a pure white one, Floy. His fur turned white as snow. Otherwise, he was jest fine, though. When old man Bremer came back to his land the next day to see what the tornado had done to his place, Slacker was fit enough in health to bite him. Strange, that didn't seem to bother Bremer much. He was a changed man. He told us somethin' very, very remarkable. You see, his house had landed on the exact same spot our house had been on. Ruby Nell told him that it was the great hand of fate that the houses had done that.

"And now Bremer said that this is what his wife had said too, and that from now on he'd listen to her and keep the peace with Texans who had been Confederate minded. He said that she had said they ought to live over where they were, and we ought to live where we were and not ever try to move the two houses. We'd jest switch farms, because it would be too much to expect another big blow that would put 'em back where they started from again.

"Next, Mr. Bremer asked us about Jim Chester, and we had to tell him of his sorrowful death by veranda. Bein' very honest, we gave him half of the pork from his hog. He was too sad to ask us for all of the meat. He'd set great store by that prizewinnin' brute. The death of Jim Chester took so much heart out of Bremer that he turned into a decent man. He was nice to his wife and kids, and he started goin' to church every Sunday. The man who owned the farm we was rentin' got together with Bremer, and they switched the ownership of them two farms on the record books at the county seat. As long as we stayed there, which wasn't too long because we got drove out by a plague of grasshoppers, Bremer never come near us again or put up barbed wire across the road, thanks to that big blow."

"That's nice, Rudd," said Grandmother. She got up. "Carolina, I think it's time we started the dishes." She turned in the doorway. "Rudd, you are the big blow—not that tornado."

"I did have a dog named Slacker and a friend named Clee Puttiphut, Susie!"

"So you did." And she went out of the room, laughing.

10
Yellow Sky Woman

I picked up Mom's and Grandmother's coffee cups and went out behind the ladies. I found them with their arms around each other, laughing. "He fooled us good and proper, Susannah," Carolina Hemmrich was saying. "He knew we had expected to hear the true story finally, but that one he jest told has to be the craziest one I've ever heard him tell." She caught sight of me and asked, "Merle, what did you think of that tale about the tornado?"

I shook my head as I went to the sink. "I think I still like the one best of all where he got stabbed with the knitting needle through the honeysuckle. Then I like the Texas Ranger one too." As I put the cups down, I asked, "Do you suppose Ruby Nell knew the real story, Mrs. Hemmrich?"

"I don't know. I never asked her, Merle. Remember, I came here to live after she passed away. I didn't know her at all well while she was Mrs. Rudd Quiney. Let me see." She paused, frowning. "My late husband died in 1877, so I left the Comanche Indian reservation soon thereafter. For some years to make a living I taught music—voice and piano—in a number of Texas towns; then in 1900 I came here to keep house for Hoyt and

Rudd. Ruby Nell died just the year before. It was of pneumonia fever."

"One thing we know for certain, Carolina," Grandmother said. "When I saw Rudd in 1875 before I left the home ranch, he had both parts of both ears. But when he came out to San Diego in 1881, part of one ear was missing. So—however he really lost it—he lost it between 1875 and 1881. Yes, indeed, it's nice to have *some* facts regarding my brother Rudd."

"What'll I do for the rest of the day?" I asked.

"Help us make watermelon-rind pickles if you want to," offered Mrs. Hemmrich.

I sighed. I'd made those pickles before. It was messy, sticky work. But when she said I could make a pecan pie if I'd rather, I brightened up a lot. We sure had a lot of pies at this place. That was because the Quiney brothers would rather eat pie than anything else. A little later, while I was using the nutcracker on the pecans, I made a decision.

I'd had my way when I'd asked right out for Brownie to sleep in the guest room. Well, I was going to ask Great-uncle Rudd another question straight to his face. If he said no to me, I'd keep telling myself we had only one more day to stay there. I knew for sure that we would be going Wednesday morning. Mom's wrist was a lot better now, though she still wore the bandage on it and soaked it.

I thought about my question all night out in the car and how I planned to ask it when I came in to breakfast. The minute I sat down at the table on that sunny, clear morning I said, "Great-uncle Rudd, aren't you *ever* going to tell us the real story of how you lost part of your ear? We're leaving tomorrow, and maybe we'll never see you again. You know that we don't believe any of those you've told us already."

"Don't you believe any one of 'em either, Tuck?" the old man asked.

"No, I don't."

"Do you want to hear the real story too?"

"Yes, I do."

"Maybe you won't find it as interestin' as the others."

Mom said quickly, "We'll take our chances, Uncle Rudd."

"All right, folks. I'll go over it in my mind and tell it to you right after supper. But every one of you has to be around to hear me tell it. It ain't any everyday story."

"Oh, I'm sure that it isn't," Mom said, as she passed Rudd the syrup for his waffles.

He took the pitcher, poured syrup over the waffles, and then before he passed it next to Hoyt, Rudd licked the spout. He winked at Graham and me because he'd heard us gasping, and he said, "This here's maple flavor. It ain't half so good or as fillin' as blackstrap molasses poured over beef tallow. Ruby Nell knowed it was my favorite dish and served it up to me all the time."

I felt sick, so sick I didn't even want my bacon. I thought my brother looked a little green, too, but Mom chuckled along with Great-uncle Hoyt, who suddenly stuck his thumb into his coffee. He remarked, "I guess this is what you been expectin' all along from Rudd and me, ain't it, kids? I bet that's what your grandma told you about the two of us—that Rudd licked the syrup jug, and I was a thumb stirrer."

Grandmother said, laughing, "I certainly did warn them about Rudd, Hoyt, but I didn't recall your using your thumb so freely."

"I didn't, Susie. I didn't till Rudd come to live with me, and then I took up the habit to save poor Carolina here from havin' to wash another spoon."

The housekeeper sighed. "Hoyt, I don't fret about washing dishes, and you know it. You can just keep on doing it. I won't let you or Rudd vex me. You don't vex your sister either. No matter what, we are determined to love both of you. We know that we'll be paid fourfold in Heaven for our good deeds down here. Neither of us expects anything different from you two."

"I do," I put in fast. "I expect to hear the truth about Great-uncle Rudd's ear."

"You're goin' to, Mo, you're goin' to. Jest you all hold your horses till after supper, you hear me? I made you a promise."

The rest of that day was spent washing, drying, and ironing our clothes to get them clean again for the trip, walking Brownie up and down the road for exercise, and arranging for the man who sold gasoline to come down with five-gallon cans and refill the Studebaker. He told Mom that it was the only automobile in the town so far, but there were twelve mules and one horse.

DIXON PUBLIC LIBRARY
DIXON, ILLINOIS

Graham wasn't with us all day long. He was with the great-uncles out in the barn, being permitted to curry-comb the mare. She hadn't had so much attention in a long time, according to Mrs. Hemmrich. But for all the work he did, hoping to get to ride her, he wasn't invited to and neither was I. Great-uncle Hoyt was still concerned with that warble the mare had on her back. I'd learned by now what a warble was—a hard, sore swelling made by the bite of a special fly.

Finally suppertime came, and for our last meal Mrs. Hemmrich outdid herself. We had beefsteak and fried potatoes, apple and pecan pies, and a fruit gelatin salad. The great-uncles ate everything in sight except for the gelatin. Great-uncle Hoyt poked at it with his knife, making it quiver, then he pushed it aside and ate the lettuce underneath. Great-uncle Rudd shoved the whole salad plate away and said, "Mebbe this is what you eat out in California these days, but I don't never eat Shiverin' Liz—not me and not Hoyt."

"Shiverin' Liz," repeated Graham happily, letting me know that from now on he'd refuse anything that was made out of gelatin too. That easy kind of dessert was what I could fix best.

"All right, are you ready?" Rudd Quiney asked, after Grandmother had set his first cup of after-dinner coffee in front of him.

My brother leaned forward with his elbows on the table and his chin in his hands. Mom lolled back in her chair, smiling, looking at her bandaged wrist resting on the table. Mrs. Hemmrich was already at her fancy-work while Grandmother sat, folding and refolding her napkin. Great-uncle Hoyt had lit a cigar and was puffing away.

Everyone seemed to be relaxed but me. I was sitting straight in my chair with my arms folded. I was waiting for the truth!

"We're all ready," I said.

He started. "Billy bedamned, it was truly long gone by when it happened. It was back in the year of 1879, not long after me and Clee Puttiphut and Ruby Nell had come back here to Texas from Missouri. Clee and his sister went back to live on the Puttiphut spread, but me and Earl didn't get along no better than before, so to earn some money I had to light out on Captain for northern parts. I surely hated to say farewell to dear little Ruby Nell, but she knowed it wouldn't be forever and I'd be true as true to her while I was gone. She knowed as soon as I had some money I planned to marry up with her. How I doted on that gal!

"After some ridin' around the country lookin' for work, I found myself a job as a cowboy for a two-bit rancher up on the Red River. He was a wisdom bringer, a schoolteacher, even if he was a him, not a her. He'd been teachin' up in the Indian Nations for a time, but he'd been left the ranch by some kin of his who'd died. So he give up teachin' to try his hand at ranchin'. He was a man about my size, with hair somethin' my color of red, but other than that we wasn't at all alike. He had his nose in a book all the time. Worse than that, he was even writin' one. It was about Indians, because he'd taught school in the Indian Nations."

"Oh, Rudd, what was his name?" Mrs. Hemmrich looked up quickly from her embroidery.

"Elbert somethin' or other. I forget what else."

The housekeeper nodded. "There was an Elbert Smith who wrote a book about Comanche Indians, as I recall."

"That'd be him. Well, I said it was a two-bit ranch with only twenty, thirty head of cows, though there was grazin' enough for lots more. There wasn't a bunkhouse at all. I had to sleep in the same little sod-built house with Elbert. By Gatlin's, how that man could snore—worse than Hoyt even!"

As Hoyt chuckled, Rudd went on. "Well, sir, one night him and me went to bed with me so weary that I didn't mind his snorin' in the same room one bit. You see, the house was jest one room for doin' everythin' in. I went to bed in my red long-john underwear and my shirt, as always, thinkin' to wake up in the next a.m. as usual, put on my hat and my vest and coat, pants, and boots, and go to work. But I never did. I woke up in the pitch blackness of that house to find myself bein' carried out of it. Yep, I could hear old Elbert snorin', but I couldn't let out one yip or yelp myself to let him know that I was very unwillingly leavin' the place. That was because of the big hand that was over my mouth. You see, I was in the process of bein' kidnapped.

"By the light of the moon outside I had my first sight of my kidnapper. He was a great, big, young Indian dressed in a fringed buckskin shirt, leggin's, and beaded moccasins. Judgin' from the way his hair was center-parted with a white streak painted down the middle, his elk-tooth and bear-claw necklaces, and them long, shiny earrings, I'd fallen into the hands of a Comanche brave. I should say fallen into the *arms* of a Comanche, because that's how he had me, holdin' me mighty tight, crushin' the breath out of me. He hauled me kickin' and thrashin' but silent to where he had two ponies waitin' not far from the river. Then he let go of my mouth but still held the knife he had to my Adam's apple. *'Silencio,'* he said. I knowed that Spanish word from my days down by the Mexican border with the Texas Rangers, so I kept quiet and let him tie my hands behind my back. Then he boosted me up onto one of the ponies, and I rode away with him, not out of choice and badly missin' my hat and my boots.

"That Comanche had come and got me without makin' a sound, and he took me away the same way. My disappearin' like that musta give old Elbert a big surprise in the mornin'."

Mrs. Hemmrich commented, "Not if Mr. Smith knew anything about Comanches. They've been known to steal horses out of a corral on a U. S. Cavalry post under a sentry's nose. It's a way they prove their courage and manhood."

"It's a good way to get hung in Texas," added Great-uncle Hoyt.

"That's so," agreed Great-uncle Rudd. "The Texas Rangers have caught and hung with pleasure a goodly number of horse rustlers. Now that big Comanche Indian had the reins of my pony, too, and he hauled me behind him over the prairie for the rest of the night and all the next day and night till noon. He give me water and some dried buffalo meat, but that was all. He wouldn't answer anythin' I asked him, either because he didn't want to or he couldn't understand the English language. I didn't know Comanche, and with my hands tied behind my back I couldn't do any sign language with him, and for a fact I didn't know much of that lingo.

"His destination was what I'd feared—a Comanche camp—and my heart was down to the soles of my bare feet when we rode in. The screechin' and howlin' there was terrible. They was greetin' him with joy because of his capturin' me, and they was greetin' me because they planned to kill me by torture. At least, that was what I thought most of them Comanches was thinkin', and so was I. I only hoped that they'd make short work of me and not make me suffer too long, but more'n likely they'd stick lances in me and shoot me full of arrows all day and the next day too, until I was a goner finally.

"But to my surprise they didn't string me up by my arms and legs. Nope, they took me to the big buffalo-hide lodge in the center of the camp. I figgered that had to be the chief's tepee, and so it was. It was the lodge of Two Knives, the chief of a band that was supposed to be on a reservation but got tired of livin' on it and rode off to hunt buffalo the way they always used to.

"The flap of the tepee was open, so Fightin' Horse, the young Indian who'd captured me, hauled me off my pony and went inside after he'd called out some words and been answered. Comanches don't jest bust in on each other in lodges. Two Knives was in there with some other old men. He was white-headed, big, and heavy.

"Now Two Knives asked us somethin'. It was only one word, *'Profesor?'* Fightin' Horse said something that had to be *yes* in Comanche, and he took out his knife and cut my hands loose. Next Two Knives asked me some words I could understand. He pointed at me and said, 'You schoolteacher?' They turned out to be the only English words he knew.

"Oh, I surely shook my head at that! And now you should of heard the uproar. Two Knives was so mad with fury he was fit to be tied. He spouted a river of Comanche at the Indian who'd stole me, and while he was spoutin' I figgered out what had happened. Fightin' Horse musta gone out to get Elbert Smith, who's been a real wisdom bringer, but he'd got hold of me in the dark by mistake. He'd done a very bad thing!"

"That's right," said Mrs. Hemmrich. "Comanche chiefs don't take kindly to members of their tribe making foolish errors." She pulled her thread through the linen with a buzzing sound and nodded.

"Why did the chief want a schoolteacher?" asked my brother.

"So's he could have his two sons learn to read and write, Tuck. Two Knives figgered if they learned the white man's language good, they'd know as much as the white man did and could outwit him at his own games. Don't think for a minute that Indians ain't smart. Some Comanches had spotted the redheaded teacher in the schoolhouse where he'd been teachin' white kids in the Indian Nations. They'd told Two Knives about him. Two Knives had had Elbert trailed down into Texas, and he'd kept his braves watchin' all the time, though Elbert never knowed he was bein' watched, and me neither. Even now it makes me shiver to think of them black Comanche eyes watchin' me every time I rode out to mend a fence. Two Knives had waited till his littlest son was old enough to benefit from schoolin', then he struck, sendin' somebody big and strong to kidnap the schoolteacher.

"The way it turned out, the chief seemed to want to find out what I was fitted for—if it wasn't for teachin' school. If I coulda wrote anythin' but my own name, believe you me, right then and there I woulda scratched the whole alphabet on the dirt floor of the lodge and tried to give Two Knives the idea that I was a wisdom bringer. It was downright dangerous not to be. But I couldn't make him think I was. I didn't know the alphabet. So I showed him how a cowboy used a lasso. Two Knives understood what I was tryin' to tell him.

He didn't need no cowboys. You coulda heard him snortin' in disgust all over the camp. Now he made a move with his hand to get me out of his lodge after he gave Fightin' Horse a wicked look that shoulda petrified a rattlesnake at ten paces.

"Fightin' Horse took me out fast, but as I went away with him I noticed the two Comanche gals sittin' cross-legged in the back of the chief's lodge. They had to be either the chief's wives or his daughters."

"Wives?" asked Graham.

"Yep, Comanches could have more'n one wife, Tuck. The richer a man was the more wives he had to work for him, tannin' hides and combin' and oilin' his long hair."

"Disgusting as it sounds, that was all too true," said Mrs. Hemmrich with a sniff.

Great-uncle Rudd went on. "They wasn't the chief's wives. For a fact, he had three wives. All three of them was elsewhere at the time. One of the gals I saw was Two Knives' daughter, Buffalo Calf Creek Woman. The other one was Yellow Sky Woman, his stepdaughter. Yellow Sky Woman was the daughter of his second wife, who was from the Cheyenne tribe. The Cheyennes were cousins of the Comanches."

"Oh, yes," said Mrs. Hemmrich over her embroidery. "The Cheyenne are a fine people—proud, generous, hard-working, honest, sober, modest, friendly, and very strong-willed."

"Mebbe all them good things are true, Carolina. All

I can truly say for that Cheyenne gal, Yellow Sky Woman, was that she was danged strong-willed. She set her cap for me the minute she set eyes on me. She wasn't one bit like them other young Comanche fillies that were slim and purty like Buffalo Calf Creek Woman. She wasn't so young in the first place, and in the second she carried some tallow and with it more muscle than I ever saw on a gal in my life before. As I said, she cottoned to my good looks as I went out of the chief's lodge to Fightin' Horse's tepee, which wasn't half so fine a lodge. And she wasn't the only female who took to me. So did purty little Buffalo Calf Creek Woman.

"You bet I left Two Knives lodge prayin' to my Maker that the Comanches wouldn't kill me now that they had no use for me. As I was layin'—tied hand and foot—on the ground in bad-tempered Fightin' Horse's lodge the next mornin', I heard the sound of voices approachin'. I felt that my last moments might be comin' up fast when I saw old Two Knives come inside. I was sure I was a goner then, but behind him came Yellow Sky Woman dressed up more like a brave than a gal. There wasn't no skirt on her. Beneath her buckskin shirt she had on leggin's like a man. She come up to me, stared at me, rolled me over with one foot, and said somethin' to Two Knives and Fightin' Horse.

"Whatever she said pleased old Fightin' Horse but not the chief, who glared at her. She glared back, and then he left the tepee, which let me know she'd got her way. Yellow Sky Woman cut the thongs that tied my feet and hands, grabbed me by the shirt collar, and started draggin' me out of Fightin' Horse's tepee.

" 'Hey, I can walk. Where are you takin' me?' I yelled at her, as I got up in spite of her pullin' and haulin'.

"That big, strong Indian gal grabbed me by the arm, jerked me along with her to a tepee a couple of doors from the chief's, and pushed me inside. There was a thin little man in there sewin' on some leather. I could see right off that he was crippled, because one of his legs was withered away. He didn't appear to be Comanche, and he wasn't. He asked me, *'Señor, habla usted Español?'*

"I knew what that meant, so I said, 'Nope, I don't talk enough Spanish to speak of. Can you talk English, mister?'

" '*Si, señor,* a little. I am Ramón.' He smiled at me. 'The woman chief wants you to be her husband *numero dos.* I am *numero uno.*'

" *'What?'* Yellow Sky Woman had gone away by now. On my hands and knees I looked out the tepee flap to see if the coast was clear and I could escape, but there was Comanches all around me, women cookin' and kids chasin' dogs and playin' games and men ridin' past on ponies. Nope, I surely couldn't escape.

" '*Si,* Yellow Sky Woman is a great woman chief.' Ramón sounded proud. 'My wife hunts buffalo and raids for horses and takes the scalps of many enemies. She is rich. She owns many horses.'

"I came back on my hands and knees to squat beside

Ramón, her number-one husband, and ask him, 'Why's she after me when she's already got you? She gives me the willies.'

"He smiled. 'Because, *señor,* no Comanche will court her. So she gets husbands who are not Comanches because she wants husbands. She will pay Fighting Horse six ponies for you. That is very many ponies.'

"I asked him, 'Ramón, what did she pay for you?'

" 'Ah, *señor,* she captured me herself, along the Rio Grande in Mexico. She carried me off while I was on my way to church.'

" 'Holy Gatlin's, what's goin' to happen to me?' I flopped down next to him, feelin' lower than a ironed-out snake.

"Ramón nodded. He sure was a cheerful galoot. 'You are going to get married, *señor*. If not to Yellow Sky Woman perhaps to Buffalo Calf Creek Woman, who likes you too.' He sounded mournful. 'I do not see what they see in you.' He smiled at my striped shirt and my long red underwear.

" 'I don't see what they see in me either,' I told him. Then I asked, 'How come you talk English so good?'

" 'I worked in a hotel in Yuma in Arizona Territory.'

" 'Oh, do you read and write?'

" 'Alas, no, *señor*. I was in the kitchen of the hotel.'

"I had an idea. 'What if you tell the chief that I have a wife already?'

"He gave me a look and shook his head. 'He will say you should have another wife.'

"I asked, 'What if I tell him I'd rather have Buffalo

Calf Creek Woman? Didn't you jest say she hankers after me, too?'

" 'No, *señor,* if you tell Two Knives that, you will make much trouble for yourself with Yellow Sky Woman and with Fighting Horse.'

" 'Why with him? Isn't he getting six horses for me?'

" '*Señor,* he loves Buffalo Calf Creek Woman. Would you know about love?'

" 'Sure I do. It ain't a comfortable emotion at times. I fancy a little old gal down home with the front name of Ruby Nell. Ain't there no way of keepin' me from marryin' up with your wife?'

" 'No, *señor,* Yellow Sky Woman has decided.'

"Well, I'd decided too. I didn't want to be jabbed to death or shot full of arrows, but I didn't want to be husband number two to nobody—particularly to a female who went out scalpin'.

"I didn't know what to do and neither did old Ramón, and then as I thought it come to me that if I had to get married, I'd rather have Buffalo Calf Creek Woman, who'd seemed peaceable enough on first sight, and I'd take my chances with Fightin' Horse not likin' me because of that. He didn't like me much already. It seemed to me that he blamed me for not bein' the schoolteacher. That wasn't my fault.

"I said to the Mexican, 'How can I get to see Buffalo Calf Creek Woman and tell her she stole my heart away? It was love at first sight for me. I'll hitch up with her.'

"As he reached for the crutch behind him, he said,

'I will tell her mother and she will tell her and then she will tell Two Knives.'

"This was too many *she's* for me, but I didn't care as long as the chief got told. I went to the flap of the tepee again and watched Ramón limp away. It seemed to me he was on my side.

"He came back purty soon frownin' like he'd got some bad news. As he came inside the lodge, he told me, 'Two Knives asks to know how many horses you can give him for that daughter?'

"I exploded with, 'Holy snakes, the only horse I own is mebbe a hunderd miles away from here. I thought the gal had taken a fancy to me. How come I ain't been asked to give Two Knives any horses for Yellow Sky Woman?'

" 'She is a brave and a woman chief, and she is giving Fighting Horse ponies for you. It is not the same, *señor*.' He looked at me like I was loco.

"After I'd sat ponderin' the fix I was in while Comanche kids kept comin' up to peek in at me in my red underwear, giggle, and run away, I had me another idea. I asked Ramón, 'I take it you can talk Comanche good enough for Fightin' Horse to understand you, too?'

" '*Sí,* I can. I have lived here for some years. Fighting Horse is sitting outside his lodge, asking a horned toad where he can find buffalo.'

"Now I looked at the Mexican like he was loco. He got my meaning and said, 'You see, *señor,* the direction the horned toad takes is the direction Fighting Horse will ride out to hunt. The horned toad has not moved yet that I know of. I will bring Fighting Horse to you once the horned toad has moved.'

"Finally the horned toad moved, and Ramón brought the big Comanche back to Yellow Sky Woman's lodge. Fightin' Horse sat across from me and scowled while Ramón told him in Comanche what I'd told Ramón in English. I wanted Fightin' Horse to know the truth —that I didn't want to marry either of them gals and that I had me a sweetheart elsewhere. Now I played my ace card, sayin' that if Fightin' Horse helped me escape, he wouldn't have no worries about losin' his gal. But he come back by sayin' that he needed them six ponies he was goin' to get from Yellow Sky Woman for me. It turned out that he was goin' to give them to Two Knives to marry Buffalo Calf Creek Woman. That didn't set so good with me, so I told Ramón to tell the Comanche that I was a famous courter of ladies down in Texas, and no gal could ever resist me. If he didn't help me get away, I'd woo his Buffalo Calf Creek Woman like I'd never wooed any gal before."

"Did he laugh, Rudd?" asked Grandmother all at once. She was smiling.

"Nope, Susie, though I agree that he should have. I was no wooer at all. He was upset and riled so he got up and left. After that Yellow Sky Woman come back with some other females. She made me get up and stand against some hides, holdin' out my legs and arms and feet. Sure as could be, I was bein' measured for some Comanche weddin' clothes.

"After that in came two men who were bigger than

I was. They pulled me out of the tepee and held me by the arms, forcin' my head back so I was lookin' into the sun and had to close my eyes. Then a old woman standin' by with a awl stepped up to me and, quick as a wink, stuck that awl through each of my ears. It didn't hurt much then at all, but the next day when she put some long seashell earrings in them, it pained like fury. It didn't ease my pain knowin' that Ramón had had the same thing done to him jest after I had. Some traders from Old Mexico had come to the camp with shells and silver, and Yellow Sky Woman had got some jewelry for her husband-that-was and her husband-to-be.

"I was gettin' desperate by now. The women were done with sewin' my weddin' suit and were puttin' beads on it and on my moccasins. It'd be any day now I'd be a wedded man. Try as I might, I couldn't figger any way of gettin' near enough to Buffalo Calf Creek Woman to court her, and truthfully I wouldn't have knowed how to begin. And that gal never come seekin' me. Ramón said she was fickle and scared of Yellow Sky Woman, and that her pa had liked them six ponies Fightin' Horse had give him to get her as his bride.

"So I sat mighty sore-eared in the tepee, listenin' to Ramón tellin' me about how the Comanches did things so I could be a good husband number two to Yellow Sky Woman. I heard about the Comanches' friends. They were the Cheyenne and the Kiowa and the Kiowa-Apaches. Their enemies were the Tonkawa. I heard about the important Comanche bands, the Yamparika and Kotsateka, Quahadi, Penateka, and the Nokomi.

From what Ramón said, they believed there was a heaven up in the sky in the east. They were scared of measles, which made me wish I was more freckled than I was, so I could make 'em think I was a measly, sick man.

"Finally, while I was only half hearin' Ramón ramblin' on and on, somethin' he said give me the first hope I'd had for days. 'Ramón,' I asked, 'are you willin' to help me in what I'm fixin' to do to get away from here?'

" 'It depends on what that is, *señor.*'

"I told him then, and he agreed to help me." Great-uncle Rudd went on again after he got his tobacco plug out. "Well, sir, that very mornin' I started to work on my idea. I laid myself down on some buffalo robes at the back of the tepee and stopped eatin' or drinkin' anythin'. Now and then I'd let out as awful a groan as I could, like I was in great pain. Naturally Yellow Sky Woman, who doted on me, got upset and sent for the medicine man, who asked Ramón if I'd told him what was wrong with me or where I hurt?

"Now good old Ramón did what I wanted him to. You shoulda seen the way that woman and the old medicine man stared at one another. You coulda knocked their eyes off with a board, they bulged out so. All at once both of 'em stepped back away from me like I'd been a sidewinder rattlin', ready to strike. And all I'd told the Mexican to tell the Comanches was that I was ill and pinin' away, because I hadn't had any of the food I craved and needed above everything else there was. I'd told Ramón to tell 'em too that there was all kinds of what I hankered after in the worst way runnin' loose around the camp. Yet I hadn't been offered one tasty bite of it. If Yellow Sky Woman truly loved me, she'd roast one of them little fat, brown puppy dogs the chief owned. Mebbe, if she done that, I'd get over my sickness. Ramón told the Comanches that I'd been raised on pup down in Texas. Pup was the victual I was most fond of. It had kept me healthy all my life."

"Ugh!" Mom made a face, then grinned at me, sitting with my arms still folded across my chest.

Great-uncle Rudd went on. "Well, sir, the more Ramón talked about pup, the more them Indians backed away from me. You see, if there was one thing the Comanches wouldn't eat, it was dog. They believed that there was a coyote god, and because of that god they'd never harm a coyote. And because a dog was a coyote's cousin, they wouldn't ever kill a dog. They went so far as to believe that anybody who ate dog was eatin' his own grandma."

"Good heavens!" came from Mom.

"Rudd's right about that, Floy," said Mrs. Hemmrich.

"All right, sir," Great-uncle Rudd plowed on, "my idea surely worked. Yellow Sky Woman and Two Knives and everybody else wanted to get rid of me. They took away them fancy earrings and gave my weddin' clothes to somebody else, I guess. They didn't kill me, though I was somewhat worried about that. Ramón explained why they didn't. Sacrificin' a dirty dog eater wouldn't bring good luck to the tribe in huntin' or war. Nobody came near Ramón and me until

Fightin' Horse come back from buffalo huntin' where he hadn't done so good. Two Knives told him to take me back where he'd found me. But first Fightin' Horse had to give back six ponies to Yellow Sky Woman, because she wasn't havin' the pleasure of my company no more and wouldn't be marryin' me. Fightin' Horse was in a fix now. He couldn't give back them six ponies to her, because he'd given them to Two Knives already for Buffalo Calf Creek Woman, who was now his wife. He wasn't a rich man. All he had to give back to Yellow Sky Woman was three crowbait ponies he had. She didn't want to take 'em, but Two Knives made her take 'em. Fightin' Horse owed her three more.

"So both Yellow Sky Woman and Fightin' Horse was in sour tempers when Fightin' Horse and me set off for Elbert's ranch. He wasn't no more pleased than I was when a day's ride out from the Indian camp, Yellow Sky Woman come suddenly gallopin' up to us wavin' a lance, yellin' and screechin' like a Comanche, though she was a Cheyenne.

"Her and Fightin' Horse talked for a while, then he reined his pony aside so she could ride up to me and fling her arms around my neck. Naturally, I figgered she wanted a good-bye kiss to show she still hankered after me, even if I was a dog eater.

"But it wasn't no kiss that fierce woman gave me. It wasn't one bit friendly the thing she did to me at that moment. Them teeth of hers clamped down on the bottom of my left ear and met through it. She bit it clear off me. But jest before she did that terrible thing, she hissed one word into my ear. It was *embustero.*

"Ramón had told her! He'd told her *everything.* That was the Spanish word for *liar.* It was one I had heard before.

"After Yellow Sky Woman had wounded me sorely, she turned her pony around and rode off over the prairie once more, shoutin' and shakin' her lance. I told myself I was lucky that she hadn't took my scalp and had been contented with part of one ear.

"That was the last I ever saw of that gal. Three days later, in a night that was darker than the inside of a cow, Fightin' Horse dumped me bound and gagged out in front of Elbert Smith's sod house. Old Elbert did seem a mite surprised to see me the next mornin' at that, but I never would tell him about how I'd left in the first place or how I'd come back. I figgered he wouldn't truly believe me.

"I never set eyes on Fightin' Horse again neither, though lots of times in the years that went by I wondered how him and Buffalo Calf Creek Woman got along and if he ever paid back the three ponies he owed to Yellow Sky Woman. And now that's the end of my tale!"

Epilogue

"Boy!" I jumped to my feet and ran out of there. Had I ever been fooled again! I didn't want to hear the others laughing at me. But their laughter came floating behind all the same.

In the kitchen I waited, fuming, until Grandmother came out with Mrs. Hemmrich. Then I said, "Grandmother, he's a terrible old man. I'll bet he doesn't even know when he's lying anymore."

"Oh, I think Rudd knows that, Merle."

"Well, you may think so, but I don't. Grandmother, what did he do in San Diego that time he got out of your sight?"

She sat down at the kitchen table, still smiling, though I couldn't see why. She put her hand to her cheek and said, "All right, I'll tell it at last and wipe the record clean. Rudd proposed marriage to three of my best friends who were without sweethearts at the time he was visiting us. He made the girls keep his asking them a secret from me. Two of the poor dears accepted him. The third one had better sense. Rudd had told all three that he was a rich cattleman and rancher. Though his earlobe was gone even then, he didn't talk about it, and we were all much too polite in those days to come straight out and ask him. Times have changed for the worse in some ways. I hinted once and was told by him to mind my own business. Rudd told the girls he was rich to make himself important, of course. The other thing he did was set fire to the parsonage of our church by letting his cigar butt drop into the cushions of the minister's sofa. The minister lost a whole room of furniture to the fire."

"But what did he do to get in trouble with the police? He didn't set the parsonage on fire on purpose, did he?"

"No, of course, he didn't do that, Merle. What he did do was get very drunk down at the waterfront. Then, because he felt far from Texas and lonesome, he stole a horse to go riding about town on. It was a policeman's horse he stole. Though to give my brother credit, he didn't know that it was."

Mrs. Hemmrich chuckled. "So that's what he did out there. I suspected he'd someday wind up as a horse thief."

"Well, in a small way he was. We put him back on the train for Texas before he sobered up. We were afraid he'd get into more trouble. We had to pay a whopping fine because of that policeman's horse. Mr. Fawcett and I moved to Pasadena right afterwards, because one of the girls Rudd proposed to, and thereby disappointed, was the daughter of Mr. Fawcett's boss."

"Oh, my!" said Carolina Hemmrich. "No wonder you left town."

"And we'll be leaving here in the morning while everything's still sweetness and light, I hope," said

Grandmother. "Merle"—she turned to me— "you've heard Rudd's final story. What did you think of it?" She was grinning at me, which made her look something like him. The Quineys had sort of the same smile.

I said, "I think it's the craziest one yet. I think he has to be the meanest tease I've ever known. I'm not going to speak one more word to him ever again."

I kept my vow too. I avoided Great-uncle Rudd until next morning when I had to come inside for our last breakfast in that house. I kept my eyes on my plate and wouldn't lift my head to look at him, even though Mom had told me I was being rude and my brother had said out in the car the night before that I was being dumb about nothing. I figured that I might be teaching the old liar something. I only wished that one story out of all of the stories he'd told had been the real truth. I wanted it to be one of those stories in which some lady had got even with him—the one about the girl and the knitting needle, the outlaw girl, the Indian girl, or even the female grizzly bear. I'd like to bite his billy be-damned ear off myself by now.

It was sunny that morning; later on it would be hot. Graham and I were sitting at the table in our traveling clothes, and the sun shone down through the window onto the backs of our necks, making me warmer than I wanted to be. I was already plenty hot under the collar about my great-uncle without needing that much sun-shine too.

Great-uncle Hoyt said to Grandmother, "You know,

Susie, when the sun hits their heads jest right, like it's doin' now, you can see the red in the kids' hair. Yes, siree, them two has Quiney blood in 'em all right. Jest lookin at 'em anybody would know they was the right kind of colts."

"Thank you, Hoyt, I'd hoped you'd like them. I'm very proud of my grandchildren."

Graham kicked me, and I kicked him back to keep him quiet, because there might be more compliments coming.

All Great-uncle Rudd said while everybody waited for him to say something nice about us too was, "They'll do. So will your gal, Floy. And come to think on it, Susie's dog ain't so bad neither, though as far as I could see, it never growed up to proper dog size."

"Thank you for those kind words, Uncles," came from Mom.

And then breakfast was over. Everyone went out to the car to say good-bye to us. Grandmother and Mrs. Hemmrich had tears in their eyes as they hugged and kissed one another. Then Mrs. Hemmrich hugged Mom and Graham—and finally me. To me she said what she hadn't said to Graham, "I'll settle, Merle, for one neck hug now, but what I'd really like is four of those hugs, six great big squeezes, and seven kisses on the cheek."

Next Great-uncle Rudd stepped up to us. The old liar tilted back his Stetson hat and said, "So long, you California Quineys." Then he gave Grandmother and Mom a quick hug and shook hands with Graham. He didn't even offer to shake mine. He and I stood looking at each other—that was all. I was glad he hadn't stuck out his hand to me, the old whopper teller.

Last of all came Great-uncle Hoyt, who'd stood waiting behind the gate. He came slowly through it past the roses to the car. He said, "Well, it's been good to see you come, and it's good to see you go. Next time you're passin' through this way, drop in again. Don't wait for a washed-out bridge."

"We won't, Hoyt, dear. Thank you all for your hospitality," said Grandmother, kissing him on the cheek.

With her handkerchief to her face, she got into the back seat of the Studebaker, and Brownie jumped in behind her. That's when I saw the yellow roses in the silver vases. They hadn't been there earlier that morning.

Mom waved and went around the car to get behind the wheel. That left only my brother and me still outside.

Great-uncle Hoyt took my brother's hand and said, "*Adiós,* Tuck. Remember me and Rudd."

"I sure will. I'll always be Tuck from now on if I can get people to call me that back home."

"You can. Stick to thinkin' of yourself as Tuck Tucker, and you can. Now you kids come here so I can tell you a final somethin' that you might find interestin'."

We came up to him, and he bent over to say very softly behind one of his hands, "I think you ought to go over to my brother before you go and take a real good look by broad daylight at his right ear."

Tuck said, "But it's his left ear that's gone, isn't it?"

"That's so, but his right ear's interestin' too. Go pretend to hug him, and you'll see what I'm talkin' about."

"Come on, Mo." Before I could say, "Not on your life, I won't!" he had me by the hand and was hauling me over. He hugged old Rudd all right—but not me. I hung back while he was doing the hugging, though I was busy all the same. I was staring.

Great-uncle Rudd's right ear had the sun shining behind it. Of course, it was pinkish because the sun was hitting it that way, but there was something strange about the ear. Yes, there *was* something to be seen. There was a little dark spot right in the middle of the lobe. I moved in closer to get a better look.

With his arms around my brother, Great-uncle Rudd looked down at me. He grinned and said, "Nope, it ain't another mole. Once upon a time it was pierced. And you never once heard me say here that I was ever a pirate, did you?"

"No, you didn't!" My eyes were glued to that right ear. All I could say now was, *"Indians? Real, true Comanche Indians!"*

As Tuck ran back to the car, my Quiney great-uncle gave me a nod, followed by a little smile. "I hope you like them yellow roses, Mo," he said.

I said, "Billy bedamned!" and grabbed him around the waist, hugging him once with all my might. Then I ran to the car as Mom honked the horn.

Author's Notes

Unlike most of my books for young readers, *Billy Bedamned, Long Gone By* has a definite moment of conception. The idea for the novel came to me during a conversation with two teachers of children's literature. While one was telling us about an in-law, a real-life Oklahoma pioneer who was missing part of one ear and who told many versions of how he had come to lose it, I decided that here was the germ of a plot for another book about my Quiney family of Texas.

Much of what I have written pertaining to the year 1929 is fact. Floy Tucker is a very daring and modern woman for that era. Her driving cross-country was a noteworthy enterprise for anyone, so much so that male motorists who did it even wrote books about their adventures on the road. I've read a number of them and made use not only of the motoring lore but also gleaned some 1920's slang. I have also consulted many magazines of the twenties, some of which would be nostalgic names to many Americans, such as *Literary Digest, Colliers', The Saturday Evening Post, Country Life, The American Magazine,* etc.

In writing of the 1870's and 1880's, I have used sources I've worked with before in my other books about the West. I've looked into the works of J. Frank Dobie, Andy Adams, and Ramon Adams. I've read what artists Frederic Remington and Charlie Russell wrote, and I found the writings of these artists as vivid as their paintings and sketches. The speech of the elderly Quiney men stems from these wonderfully colorful accounts of the Old West.

There is a lot of factual material in the tall tales Rudd Quiney relates to his family. The Civil War battle of Sharpsburg (or Antietam) is, of course, a real one, and I have tried to describe it as it might have been seen from the viewpoint of one of General Hood's wild young Texans. The incident of missing the breakfast of "frying meat" is true. It did infuriate the Texans. General John B. Hood was not a Texan but adopted the state as it has now adopted him. This much-wounded soldier died in 1879. The anecdote of the Yankee officer and the two Confederate soldiers and the much-desired new boots is a true one, though it is not connected with Sharpsburg.

Rudd's purported adventure with the grizzly bear takes place in my own part of the world. Holcomb and Bear Valleys in San Bernardino County, California, were notorious in the 1860's and up almost into the twentieth century for their large numbers of ferocious bears. They were also the locales of some gold-mining camps that contained a goodly proportion of Confederate sympathizers and former soldiers of Lee's army.

Tornadoes and cyclones are natural starting points for tall tales, as folklore testifies, and pioneer accounts and cowboy memoirs are a good source of material. The Texas Rangers and old-time outlaws are also tall-tale materials. For interesting reading, try *The Gentleman in White Hats, Dramatic Episodes in the History of the Texas Rangers* by Claude Leroy and *Capt. Lee Hall of Texas* by Dora Neill Raymond.

In some ways Rudd Quiney's last tale must seem the most unlikely of all. But it has many facts interwoven with its fiction. The depiction of Comanche life is based on a large number of sources, many of them old photographs. My chief sources were *The Comanches, Lords of the South Plains* by Ernest Wallace and E. Adamson Hoebel and *The Last Captive,* the true account of Apache and Comanche captive Herman Lehman. The lodge etiquette I describe is vouched for by eyewitness accounts. Comanches were formal about such matters. They had more than one wife and sometimes a wife from another tribe. A woman "chief," such as Yellow Sky Woman, *could* exist in that society and sometimes—though rarely—did. She could have husbands or even "wives," other women to keep her lodge for her. Like the wives of a Comanche man, they could be Mexicans, other Indians, Comanches, or whites.

The Comanches considered horses as wealth. The price of a

captive or a bride was measured in horses or ponies. Comanches had a taboo against eating dog, too, while some other Indian peoples were very fond of dog meat and refused to eat other creatures as their particular taboo. The ritual torture and death of captives was an unpleasant feature of Comanche life, as it was with other Plains tribes. It was a religious rite, a sacrifice of sorts, that was supposed to bring prosperity to the people.

Dandies among Comanche men had pierced ears and wore long, dangling earrings of seashells along with necklaces of bear claws and elk teeth. The magnificent quill and beadwork their mothers, wives, and sisters did to adorn the buckskin clothing men wore is sometimes found in museums today.

A number of people contributed some of the wildly varying pieces of information I needed to write this novel. I consulted them for everything—from how to crank a car in the late 1920's to horse behavior, astrology, and Civil War history. They are Charlotte Burton, Dina Stallings, Sue Schultz, Al Kettering, Kathleen Kuegel, Professor Hal Bridges, Julie Everett, Carrie Huber, and Joan and Jim McCrea. Two gracious Fort Worth, Texas, librarians, Patricia Chadwell and Camille Connor, supplied me with information about their exciting city in 1876.

Patricia Beatty
March, 1976

About the Author

Now a resident of Southern California, Patricia Beatty was born in Portland, Oregon. She was graduated from Reed College there, and then taught high-school English and history for four years. Later she held various positions as science and technical librarian and also as a children's librarian. Quite recently she has taught Writing Fiction for Children in the Extension Department of the University of California, Los Angeles. She has had a number of historical novels published by Morrow, several of them dealing with the American West in the 1860 to 1895 period.

With her late husband, Dr. John Beatty, Mrs. Beatty also co-authored a number of books. One of them, *The Royal Dirk,* was chosen as an Award Book by the Southern California Council on Children's and Young People's Literature. Subsequently Mrs. Beatty received another award from the Council for her Distinguished Body of Work.

Mrs. Beatty is now married to a professor of economics at the University of California, Riverside, and she has a married daughter, Alexandra Beatty Stewart.